A Selection of Eclecti Stories

Hope

Christmas day and Hope was sitting in the kitchen having her first coffee of the day, waiting patiently for her children to wake up. She couldn't wait to see Poppy and Joey open the huge pile of presents under the tree.

Ten minutes later, she heard her children walk across the landing and she walked into the hallway, and when they got to the bottom of the stairs, they followed her into the lounge. She felt pleased with herself for having got most of the things they'd wanted. It hadn't been easy, but she'd managed to put a little money aside each week.

They were squealing with delight and she laughed with them, then she reached under the tree for her present. It was from her children; courtesy of their grandmother. It turned out to be a beautiful silver locket, and when she opened it, there was a picture of Jerry and her children in it. Tears welled up in her eyes, but she kept her emotions in check. There had been too many tears shed over the last few years, now, it was time to move on.

'When are we going to nanny's?' Six-year-old Joey called out.

'Tomorrow. Today, I'm treating us to Christmas dinner down the pub.'
'Daddy's pub,' ten-year-old Poppy screamed, as she cuddled her mother.
'That's the one.'

When Jerry was alive, they would go to the pub for Sunday roast every week as a treat. After that, depending on the weather, they would go to a theme park or the cinema. She was lucky if she could afford a joint of meat these days and as for treats, they were rare.

It wasn't Jerry's fault that they hadn't had any life insurance, or the fact that neither of them had thought about putting money away. After all, neither of them expected their opposite number to die at the age of thirty.

It had been hard these last two years, relying on benefits, doing a degree and working weekends at the supermarket, but somehow, they were muddling through. Thank heaven for her mother and father who doted on the children, along with Jerry's parents who took the children off her hands occasionally.
Wiping the tears out of her eyes, she said happily, 'Who wants waffles?'

The children let out an almighty shriek, which she took as a yes, and leaving them to play with their toys she walked into the kitchen, picked up the picture of her late husband and kissed it.

Once they had washed and dressed themselves, the children spent the rest of the morning playing with their toys in the bedroom and she spent the morning making mince pies and cakes - just to keep busy. She may be feeling low, but the children were having a great time and that was all that mattered.

Just as she took the last of the mince pies out of the oven, there was a knock at the door.
'Can I come in?' her best friend Rebecca asked, as she opened the door to her.
'I hope you don't mind, but I've come for a break. Yummy, what's that smell?'
'Mince pies. Come into the kitchen and I'll make you a coffee.'
'Got anything stronger?' Rebecca asked playfully.
Hope took a miniature bottle of wine out of the fridge and poured it into a glass and said, 'This do?'
'Perfect, do you need a hand with anything?'
'No, just tidying up now. How's the twins?'
'Noisy. Ryan is looking after them and they were both crying when I left. I just had to get out of there for a bit; they're really demanding. How are you really?'

'It's Christmas, you know how it is.'
'I know. Are you still going out for dinner?' Then, feeling sorry for her best friend she stood up and hugged her.
Hope wiped the tear out of her eye, took some mince pies from the table, wrapped them in some tin foil and handing them to her said, 'Yes, and I'm going to dress up.'
'Good for you, it's about time. I loved Jerry, you know that, but you need to move on.'
'That's what mum says, but it's not that easy.'

'Aunty Becky! Can we play with the twins?' Poppy asked excitedly, as she ran over to her.

'Not now, they're due for a nap and hopefully, they'll be asleep when I get home.'
'That's what babies do,' Hope said sympathetically, after seeing her daughter's disappointed face.
'You can pop in when you get back if you like?'
The children looked at their mum expectantly and Hope said, 'Alright, but only if we're home early.'
Rebecca stayed for another ten minutes and would have stayed longer, if her in-laws weren't due any minute.

'How are you Hope?' The manager asked, as they walked into the pub.
'We're all good thank you Harry.'
'My, the children have grown. We've missed seeing you in here.'
'That's very kind of you.'
'Come this way, I've put you by the play area.'
'Good thinking, thanks.'
That was kind, Hope thought, as they made their way to the back of the room.

As Hope watched her children play, she suddenly felt isolated. She had come out to have an enjoyable time, not to be hidden away at the back of the room. Socially, this wasn't good for her or the children.

While the children played in the ball pool, Hope looked for Harry, and five minutes later she found him behind the bar, eagerly devouring a mince pie.
'May I have a word?'
'Sure,' he said, as he wrapped his mince pie in a napkin.
'I appreciate why you've given us that table, but I really need to be around people. Any chance I could be moved?'
'Wait here, I'll see what I can do, be right back.'

Hope fetched the children from the play area, with a promise that they could return later, and they were now standing by the bar.

Five minutes later, Harry returned and said happily, 'You're in luck, there's a place over by the window, we've had a cancellation.'
She was glad that she was at a different table but sad that somebody had cancelled - on Christmas day of all days.

The meal was delicious and when they'd finished eating, the children went back to playing in the ball pool and were lucky enough to meet up with some friends from school, which allowed Hope to spend some time on her own. Knowing that the children were happy, Hope decided to treat herself to a glass of wine.

'Hey,' a young man in a rugby shirt and shorts said, as he walked by. It was Brian, a good friend of Jerry's, and she smiled up at him as he took a step back and sat opposite her.
'How are the children?'
'Good, well, you know?'
Brian nodded.
'I keep meaning to pop by, but I don't seem to have the time.'
'It's Ok.'
'No, it's not. I'll call around in a couple of weeks,' he replied, and feeling uncomfortable, he stood up and said, 'Anyway, I've got to go, a few of us are having a kick around this afternoon.'

Brian had been Jerry's best friend since primary school and suddenly, he was acting as if he hardly knew her, and she was annoyed. For the children mostly, for Jerry and Brian would often take the children to watch their local football team play and the children loved him. He was almost like an uncle to them. Thank god they hadn't seen him, or god knows how they would have reacted.

'Hey?'
Hope looked up at the man standing beside her but didn't recognise him and said,' I'm sorry, do I know you?'
'Sadly, no. This was my table. I called to cancel but changed my mind, and it looks like Harry's given it to you. No worries, I'm sure he'll find me another one.'
'Dad!' a teenage boy grunted, as he walked up to the table. 'Harry has moved us to the back of the room now, I told you not to cancel,' he said angrily.
'I thought you didn't want to come,' his father said in his defence, hoping his son wasn't going to make a fuss.
'I thought you didn't.'
'Crossed wires I guess,' the man said, and he cuddled his son, who squirmed in his arms and pulled away from him.

'I know where Harry has put you, it's not nice, sit here, I'll be going soon.'
'If you're sure?'
'You'll have to pull up another chair though, because my children are over there,' she said, pointing to the ball pool.
'I'm Flinn.'
'Ted is over there can I go and see him?' his son asked, and Flinn nodded and when he walked away, Flinn said casually, 'Josh would go anyway, sometimes, I wonder who the parent is.'
Hope laughed politely and took a sip of her wine.

'I'm Hope, pleased to meet you.'

'I hope you don't mind me asking, but where's your other half?'
'Jerry died two years ago. It was a motor bike accident. He was coming home from work and he was so tired, he forgot to put his lights on. It was dark and somebody went into the back of him.'
'I'm sorry, I didn't mean to upset you.'
'I'm not upset. I can talk about it now.'
A short silence ensued while they both tried to think of something to say.

'What do you do for a living?' she asked, trying to break the silence.
'I'm an architect. You?'
'I work in a supermarket at the weekend and I'm studying in the week.'
'Cool. Would you like another drink?'
'No thank you, as soon as the kids have had enough, I'll be taking them home. It's been a long day - for all of us.'
'I'm sorry, if you'll excuse me, I need to find out where my son has got to. His mother will kill me if I don't feed him.'
Hope watched him walk away and smiled, he was a good-looking man, and it felt nice to chat to somebody of the opposite sex.

'Mum,' Joey said, as he plonked himself on the seat by the window. 'Can we stay and play with our friends for a bit?'
'Sure, where's your sister?'
'Playing with Molly.'
'Come on,' Hope said happily, 'Let's go and see what she's up too.'

Hope stood watching them play for a while and when she got back to her table, Flinn and Josh were tucking into their dinner and not wanting to be in the way she said, 'I'll see you around guys,' and went to walk away, when Flinn asked her to sit down.

'You've got another drink coming, stay and natter. Josh is going to his mother's after dinner and I could do with the company.'

'If you're sure?'

'He's sure,' Josh said, and she smiled and sat down.

Ten minutes later, Josh was heading home, but not before hugging his father and making sure he was still taking him to the match on Sunday.

'He's a good lad,' he said, only half believing it.

'Have you any other children?'

'No. I would have liked more, but she didn't. You never know, I might have more one day.'

'Anything's possible.'

'What about you, do you want any more?'

'I don't know, I'm happy with the two I have. I haven't actually thought about it.'

'How long has it been since your husband died?'

'Two years, I'm sure I told you that?'

'Probably, but I've got a memory like a sieve, especially when I'm facing someone as beautiful as you. You're still young. You loved him, I get that, but it's time to move on isn't it?'

Blushing, Hope said cautiously, 'That's what everyone keeps saying, but it's not that easy.'

'You need to listen to them. You're gorgeous, so you won't have any trouble finding another partner. You have to move on with your life.'

'You sound like a shrink.'

'Sorry, but for some reason, I don't like to think of you on your own.'
'I've got a good family and some great mates.'

Shrugging his shoulders and sighing he said, 'I think I may be going about this the wrong way. Look, I'm not much good at this sort of thing, but I really like you. Would you like to have coffee sometime?'
Hope blushed and was about to put him in his place when Poppy came back.
'I'm tired mum.'
Hope cuddled her and then Joey came back and asked if they could go home.
'Guys, this is Flinn.'
The children said hello in unison and Hope put Poppy's coat on, while Flinn helped Joey into his.

'Can I walk you home?'
'We're fine thanks, we don't live far.'
'Please think about what I said. I'll be here next Sunday around three if you fancy a drink?'
'I don't think so.'
'I'll be here anyway. I like you and I haven't felt this way in ages, just consider it will you?'
She kissed him politely on the cheek and said, 'I'll think about it.'
He was pleased with that, but he had no idea if he'd see her again.

As Hope walked out of the pub, she smiled to herself. Nothing was going to come of it, but it was nice to think that somebody was attracted to her, even though he was a bit forward. Anyway, even if she did want to see him again, and she was sure she did, she had to work the weekend, so it was never going to happen.

Hope had been thinking about Flinn all week, especially at night when the children were asleep. So much so, that she was starting to feel guilty. It felt as though she was being unfaithful to Jerry.

Saturday couldn't come quick enough for Hope because she'd been stuck in all week and needed a break from the children, and she was pretty sure they needed a break from her. The weather had been terrible, and she'd not been able to take them out as much as she would have liked, and they were all a little on edge.

Could This be the Start of Something?

The supermarket was extremely busy today because the sales had started, and she was constantly refilling the shelves; but she didn't mind that, because it took her mind of Flinn. The busier the better as far as she was concerned.

'Hey.'
Hope turned around and smiled - it was Flinn.
'What are you doing here?' she asked, as she whipped off her cap.
'I've come to see you.'
'How did you know I worked here?'
'I didn't. I've been around several supermarkets already.'
'I'm flattered. Or rather, I think I am, because it could come across as creepy.'
'No way. Life is too short. I like you and I think you like me, best strike while the iron is hot, how do you fancy going on a date with me?'

'I'd have to get a babysitter. My mum already has them at the weekends, so I don't really want to impose on her; and I don't actually like being referred to as a hot iron.'
'Sorry, I can be a little crass sometimes. Bring the children with you. Come to my house for dinner after work tomorrow.'
'I'm always shattered on a Sunday. Plus, I don't know if I want to start dating again.'
'Why not?'
'I'm sorry, I can't discuss this here, I'm supposed to be working.'
'When do you finish?'
'In ten minutes.'
'Meet me in the café.'
Then he walked off before she had time to say no.

Hope walked into the café and smiled when he called her over. What harm would it do to go out with him?
'I've got you a coffee, how long have you got?'
'Half an hour.'
'Shall I get you a sandwich?'
'No thanks.'
'Look, I get that you don't want to start dating, but think about it. What harm will it do?'
'I've got my kids to consider, they're still young. I'm not sure they're ready for another father figure in their life. At least not yet.'
'I can understand that. Why don't we just meet up for coffee once a week. I work from home, so I can make time to see you.'
'We could meet up once a week I suppose, and the kids wouldn't have to know.'
'That's right. What about Monday, at eleven in the pub? We could have brunch.'

'Alright, I don't see why not.'

'Good, now I've got to pick Josh up and I'm late. He used to stay over, but he's growing up fast and I only see him on Saturdays. I've no idea where the time's gone, it wasn't long ago that he was starting school.'
He kissed her on the cheek, smiled and said, 'This may sound corny and I apologise now, but you are gorgeous.'
'Thank you, now get going, I've got to get back to work.'
He saluted her, then left.

A year later

Hope stood watching her children as they played in the ball pool and smiled. A year on, and things had changed dramatically.
'Hey Hope.'
Hope turned around and kissed Flinn on the cheek and said, 'What are you doing here?'
'This is Kerry,' he said, giving her one of his trademark cheeky grins.
'Pleased to meet you Kerry,' Hope said, and smiled. She must be the fifth person he'd dated this year. Hopefully, this would be the last.
'Where's Simon?'
'He'll be along in a minute, he's running late.'
'More fool him. Leaving a good-looking woman like you sitting here all alone. Still, he's a good one.'
'I think so. Same time on Monday?'
'Of course, but don't bring Simon this time. I love the guy, but I want you all to myself.'

'Sorry Flinn, we come as a pair,' Simon said, as he walked up to Hope and kissed her on the cheek, then he put his arm around her waist and smiled.
'You're a lucky guy Simon.' Then remembering he had a date he said, 'but not as lucky as me, hey Kerry.' Then he took Kerry's hand and walked away, wishing things had worked out with Hope.

Hope smiled, she could see Kerry was falling under his spell already, just like she had once, until Simon had rescued her from his evil clutches.
'Where are the children?' Simon asked, and Hope pointed to the ball pool.
'Great, I've got something to ask you, come back to the table.'

Sitting down now, Simon took her hand in his and said, 'We've been together for nine months and I need to ask you something.'
'I don't want to marry you. I told you that last week.'
'Ouch,' he said, putting his hand on his heart, pretending to be hurt.
Hope laughed, and he got down on one knee and holding her hand in his, he whispered, 'Will you do me the honour of living with me?'
'And the children?'
'Just you. We can sell the children.'
Then he got up and sat opposite her and they laughed.

'Mum! Can we play some more?' Josh asked excitedly, as he took a big swig of lemonade.
'Of course.'
Happily, he skipped off.
'Well?' Simon asked impatiently.

'I can't take that step, not yet.'
'Yet or never.'
'Yet. Alright, I'll put it out there. I love you, but I don't want to move in with you, I'm not sure if I'm over my husband yet. Sometimes I feel a little guilty.'
'You love me?'
'I didn't mean to say that. I was waiting for you to say it first, now I feel silly.'
'How long have you known?'
'Since you dropped your coffee over me in the pub while I was waiting for Flinn.' Then, looking at him expectantly she said, 'Well?'
'Well what?'

Feeling disheartened, she stood up and said, 'I better see how the children are getting on.'
But as she went to walk away, Simon stood up, took her in his arms and kissed her on the lips, then gently pushed her from him and said, 'I was only playing with you. I love you too. If I didn't, I wouldn't have asked you to live with me, now would I?'

They both sat down, and Hope looked at him across the table as he took her hand in his. He felt terrible; he hadn't meant to upset her.
'When did you first know you loved me?' she asked expectantly.
'When you walked out of work one day. You had on your work clothes and cap and was fretting about how you looked, and I thought you looked beautiful.'
'Wow! If you think that will persuade me to marry you... You'd be right.'
'You'll marry me?'
'Yes.'

'Oh my god, when?'
'Next year, or the year after.'
'I thought there would be a catch.'
'No catch. It's going to be a big wrench for the children. You can't move in straight away, but you can start staying over at weekends, just so they get used to you. I need them to feel comfortable with you before you become their stepfather.'
'That's a terrible word. I hope I'll be more of an uncle.'
Hope smiled and said cheerfully, 'You always say the right thing.'
'I'm just being me.'
'That's why I love you.'

It had been over six months now and Simon had been staying over on Saturday night and going home Sunday evening, and things were working out great, until Becky had planted a seed in her head.

One Friday night, after their second bottle of wine, Becky had asked what Simon did for a living and where he lived, and it suddenly dawned on her, that she didn't know, and she didn't know how to contact him either. She was going to have to talk to him about that.

Having put the children to bed and read them a story, she was now sat on the settee with Simon.
'Have you got a phone number I can have? In case I have to get in touch with you.'
He frowned, looked at her and said suspiciously, 'I'm always on time, why do you want my number?'
'Just in case of emergencies.'
'Ok. I'll give it to you later. Are you alright?'
'Yes, why?'

'You seem pensive, as if you want to say something but are too scared to say it. I don't like that.'
'I'm sorry, but I've only just realised, I don't know where you live. We've been seeing each other a long time; it would be nice to go to your house occasionally.'

Suddenly, Simon went red and stood up, and looking down at her he said brashly, 'Don't you trust me?'
Looking up at him she said guardedly, 'You're being a bit defensive, are you married?'
'I don't believe this, you know me. Why are you cross examining me like this?'
'Are you going to give me a phone number and your address or not?'
'No.'
'Why?'
'I'm in between houses and I'm living in a hotel. My new house is being refurbished.'
Suddenly, alarm bells started to ring, and she said thoughtfully, 'Is that why you wanted to move in with me, so that you'd have somewhere to live?'

Of course not. How could you even think that!'
'I think it's best if you go. I've got a lot of thinking to do, I'll ring you in the week.'
Then crossly, she walked out into the hall, opened the front door and as he was about to walk out, she said sarcastically, 'Of course, I can't ring you can I, and I can't come to your house either. Do you even have a job?'

Simon desperately wanted to tell her where he lived and what he did for a living, but he was scared. Once she found out, he'd never be certain that she loved him for who he was, and not for what he had. He'd been stung before and although he didn't want to lump her in that category, he was scared.

Hope hadn't seen Simon for two weeks and she and the children were missing him, but she had to remain strong. When she'd thought about the matter some more, she realised that she hardly knew anything about him. All she really knew, was that he was a great lover and a caring man. Which was all she'd ever wanted, but for the sake of her children, she had to be sure he was legitimate.

Although she was missing him, over the next few weeks, she resigned herself to the fact that her relationship with Simon was over, and she carried on with her life as usual. It was funny, when she'd been seeing Simon, all the worries of everyday life seemed not to matter, but now, she was fretting over the smallest things.

Then, as the bills dropped through the letterbox, she realised that she'd been so wrapped up in Simon, that she'd forgotten to pay some of the bills. She had used the money to pay her way when she and Simon and the children went out, which had been every Saturday evening. It wasn't Simon's fault; she'd just been happy and had forgotten about the mundane things in life.

It took her two afternoons to sort out repayment plans for her gas, water, and council tax. Fortunately, she still had enough to live on. Thank god she still had her part time job at the supermarket; despite her ringing in sick on several occasions so that she could be with Simon. She was angry with herself for getting herself in that position and swore to herself, that it would never happen again. The last thing she needed was to get into debt.

The children were at school and after finishing one of her many assignments, Hope put her essay in the drawer and answered the door.
'Hi,' Simon said, and she couldn't help but smile at him.
'May I come in? We need to talk?'
'I've got nothing to say. Go home Simon, wherever that is.'
'Funny,' he said, annoyed with her for bringing that up.'
'I haven't seen you for ages and now you think you can just come back into our lives, but you can't. You not only let me down, you let my children down too.'
'Let me in, I wouldn't hurt you for the world.'
'It's too late. I've come to a decision. I don't want a man in my life yet. Especially one who's not being truthful with me. I let my guard down, and if it wasn't for the fact that I had sense enough to sort my bills out, me and the children could have been out on our ear.'

'If you're worried about bills, I can help you.'
'Don't be silly. Why would you do that?'
'Because I love you damn it. Why are you being like this, I thought we were getting on great. You said you loved me.'
'I do love you, but I know nothing about you... nothing?'
Simon sat down and sighed, despite his fears, he had to tell her.
'Sit down please,' he said, and she did as he asked. 'I've missed you.'
'Just get on with it.'
'Actually, let me show you. I'll take you to where I live. Are you free now?'
'I'll ring mum, she'll pick the kids up for me.'

As they drove into the gated estate, Hope couldn't believe the size of the houses in the street and she looked at him and said, 'You are joking?'
Then, he pulled into the drive of his three-storey town house and they walked up to the front door, and when an elderly lady opened the door he said, 'I forgot my key.'
'Sir,' the elderly lady said, as she led them into the dining room.
'Who's she?' Hope asked, as she sat on one of the red leather sofas.
'She's my housekeeper, she's been with the family for ages.'
'You mean like a servant?'
'Beryl isn't a servant, she's family.'
Hope frowned, and when Beryl walked in with a cup of tea for her, she took it willingly.

'Is she staying for dinner?' Beryl said unenthusiastically. Then added, 'I'm going to my sisters tonight remember.'
Simon hugged her and she brushed his cheek with the back of her hand, and he kissed her on the cheek and said, 'You get going, I can cook.'
'Yea right,' Beryl said sarcastically, as she walked out the door.
Hope laughed, Beryl was cheeky, and he was right, he didn't treat her like a servant at all, in fact, he seemed to be fond of her.

After taking a sip of tea, he put the cup down and sat on the settee with her and said, 'I'm the owner of a large retail company and luckily, it's been successful. You could say that this house is the fruits of my labour, so to speak, and I'm mortgage free, so when you move in, you won't have to pay any rent.'

'Why didn't you tell me?'
'I wanted to be sure you weren't after my money.'
'You chatted me up remember. It's a lot to take in, I want to go home.'

'Bloody hell, you can't ostracise me because I have money. If you move in with me, you'd have a great life.'
A tear came to her eye when she said, 'I don't want to move in with you yet. Not ever. If I brought my children here and they got used to this lifestyle and we finished, it wouldn't be fair on them.'
'I could buy a smaller house.'

'We're worlds apart. So, when you come to my house, you're actually slumming it.'
'I'd be happy to move in with you if you'd prefer that.'
'I would be stupid to forego this opportunity, but I've got to work out if I'm doing this because I love you, or because I have no money. After all, you've already walked out on us once.'
'Now you see why I didn't tell you. Let me take you home and you can think about it.'
'I think that's best.'

Love Conquers all, doesn't it?

Putting the towel down, Hope picked up the picture of her husband and whispered, *I love you darling, but I need to move on.* Then, she opened the drawer, put the picture inside it and wiped away the tears.

She had been seeing Simon again for the last few months, and she was grateful she'd finally come to her senses. If it worked out, then she would consider moving to his house.

For now, they were going to have a trial period in her house, and she couldn't wait. They were going to go Dutch on the bills which was a bonus, but best of all, she would be seeing him when she woke up in the morning, and to top that, this was going to be their first Christmas together as a family and she was excited.

She had wanted to go to her favourite pub, but Simon would not have it, and suggested another place, which had saddened her. However, when Simon said that they needed to make their own memories, she quickly came around to the idea.

'Simons here,' her children said in unison and she watched contentedly, as he cuddled them.
'Wow, you look good, you didn't have to dress up.'
'I didn't,' then she laughed. He was full of compliments like that and she loved that about him; especially as they were spontaneous.
'I've bought a bottle of bubbly, to celebrate you moving in.'
'That's great, but first, I need a cuppa, want one?'

Hope watched him walk into the kitchen and put the kettle on, then, as he looked in the drawer for some spoons, she walked a little closer; and when he pulled the picture of her husband out of the drawer, put it on the side and said, ' We're in this together mate,' she knew, that this would be the last time she would call this place home.

Holding Out for a Prince

Jon put the file in the cabinet, closed the drawer and put the key in his pocket and sighed. Then he sat down, shut off his computer, turned off the lamp and walked out of his cubicle to where Lori was sitting.
'Goodnight Lori,' he said, pausing for a second. He wanted to ask her out but didn't have the nerve.

Lori looked at Jon standing by the lift and sighed. He was so good looking, and she knew, that he would never look twice at her. The girls in the office loved him and he was never without a date. If she wasn't so shy, she would have asked him out for a coffee, but she didn't have the nerve. Plus, in the looks department she was nothing special compared to the girls he usually went out with.

Jon put the boxed meal in the microwave and looked at the time, it had gone seven now and he only had twenty minutes to get ready. Jane from the office had asked him out for a meal and although he liked her, he didn't really want to go. Still, it stopped him from being lonely. Yes, he had plenty of dates, but he wanted something serious now.

Lori paid a visit to her mother's then did some food shopping and reluctantly walked home. She knew it would be cheaper to shop once a week, but she was also aware, that if she did that, she'd have nothing to do in the week.

Sitting in the front room, looking down at the street below, she smiled at the que outside the cinema. There were several couples laughing and having fun, and she wished she had someone to share things with. The fact that it was a week before Christmas just made things worse, and although mum had invited her over for Christmas dinner, she had declined her offer. Her brother and sister both had partners and she knew she would feel out of place, especially as her sister was pregnant.

'Hey Jane,' Jon said, as he met up with her outside the restaurant.
'You're late,' she said politely, not wanting to upset him, for he had a reputation of being a one-night stand kind of guy and she wanted more than that.
'Yes, sorry. I had to do some overtime,' he lied.
Seeing that he was frowning, Jane changed the subject and said, 'They do a great steak here, my treat.'
'I'd rather go Dutch,' he said politely, as he followed her into the restaurant and she nodded, hoping she hadn't scared him off.

As Jon tucked into his beef wellington, he smiled at Jane and said as kindly as he could, 'I'm sorry, I don't think this is working out.'
Jane put her knife down and said miserably, 'We've only had two dates, have I done anything to upset you?'
He was about to say it's not you, it's me, but decided against it, even though it was true.
'I like you, but I'm not sure we're suited.'
'Bloody hell, Maria from accounts said you did the exact same thing to her, I should have listened to her. What exactly do you want from a relationship?'
'I wish I knew.'
She stood up, put on her cardigan, looked at him and said angrily, 'You can pay for the bloody meal. Let's call it compensation for leading me on.'

Then, she gave him a sarcastic grin and walked out of the restaurant and he put his hand in his pocket and pulled out his wallet. Somehow, the beef didn't look as tasty; especially since he'd already eaten.

'Are you going to the party tomorrow night? If you're not, I need a babysitter.'
Lori had been babysitting Susie's children for the last five years but not this time. She was going to the Christmas party tomorrow night in the hope that Jon would ask her to dance. That one dance would make her Christmas; probably her year.
'Yes, I'm going, sorry.'
'But you do it every year, now what am I going to do?'
In her head, Lori was screaming *I want a bloody life too,* but instead, she politely said, 'I'm sorry.'
Tutting, Susie walked to the lift.
'That was brave of you,' Poppy said, as she walked up to Lori.
'Brave or stupid. I've nothing to wear and nobody to go with.'
'You're going with me, my hubby can't make it this year, so you're my date.'
Lori smiled.

The night of the party and Lori had butterflies in her stomach and felt a little queasy. She pulled her black dress out of the wardrobe and laid it on the bed and screwed her nose up; it was too short and looked like it would show too much breast. She wished now that she'd tried it on in the shop, but she hadn't had that luxury, for she'd gone to the shops after work and only had half an hour to find something.

Reluctantly, she put the dress on and much to her delight she loved it, and although short, it didn't look tarty at all, and as for her breasts, luckily, having very little in that department they were lost in the material. Then, she put on her flats and rather than making the whole ensemble look dowdy, they made it look modern and she couldn't believe it; she looked pretty. She brushed her long brown hair, picked up her handbag and was just about to walk out the door when the phone rang.

'Hi, sorry Lori, I'm not going to the party tonight, Mikey has come down with the chicken pox.'
Lori told Penny not to worry and sat down by the window and kicked off her shoes. That put paid to that then, for there was no way she would be walking into the party alone.

Lori seemed to spend her life looking out of her bedroom window watching other people enjoying themselves and tonight wasn't any different. She'd been sitting there for an hour now, trying to pluck up the courage to go to the party. It wasn't as if she didn't know anyone. She liked her work mates and knew, that she would have plenty of people to talk to. It was just the initial walking into the party alone that worried her.

Jon couldn't wait to get to the party, he'd heard, that for the first time in ages, Lori was going. He'd only been at the firm for just over a year, but he'd heard that she was a shy person, very much like himself. Yes, he went out a lot with his mates and had his fair share of women, but now that he'd seen Lori, and liked her, he didn't have the courage to ask her out. He was a bit of an enigma really; what you saw on the outside wasn't the real him.

Jon had been at the party for over an hour now, and there was still no sign of her. He'd chosen to sit in the bar next door because it was quieter and having danced for most of that hour, he'd needed a break. Plus, he could see Lori walk in when she arrived. If she ever got there, for it looked like she was chickening out.

Lori stood outside the pub desperately trying to sum up the courage to go in…alone. But it wasn't happening, even though she knew that Jon was there; for she'd seen him go in.

'Is that you Lori?'
Lori looked up to see Susie looking at her and she smiled and waited for her to continue.
'My mum's babysitting, thank god. Come on, let's go in together, then it won't look so bad.'
Lori smiled and willingly walked in with her, pleased that the decision had been taken out of her hands, for she had been thinking about going home.

Jon smiled when he saw Lori walk in with Susie. Lori had left her hair down and she looked stunning. All he had to do now, was pluck up the courage to ask her to dance.

'Wow! is that you Lori, you look stunning, 'Mike from packaging said, sidling up close to her.
'Want to dance?'
Although she wasn't particularly keen on Mike, she said yes, and walked with him on to the dance floor and as he put his clammy arms around her, she could smell his sweaty armpits which made her feel sick. Suddenly, thinking she was going to throw up, she ran into the toilets

and sure enough, she was sick. What a great way to start the evening.

'Are you alright?' Susie asked kindly. Then she laughed and said, 'I guess the stench of Mike got to you too.'
Wiping her mouth and popping in a mint, Lori said, 'The man stinks, human resources need to tell him.'
Susie laughed and said, 'I am human resources remember, and we have, but he still doesn't get the message and smelling isn't an offence. Why do you think he works in packaging now?'
They both laughed until their sides hurt and ten minutes later, they were sitting with their friends from the office.

'Anybody seen Jon tonight, I'm going to ask him to dance, I fancy him like mad,' one of the women said and Lori smiled; she wasn't the only one who liked him.
'Shush, there he is, he's coming over.'
All the women, including Lori sat up straight and Lori wondered which one of her workmates he would choose. Then she slumped into the chair, what was the use of caring, he wouldn't pick her.

'Would you like to dance Lori?'
Surprised and ecstatic at the same time, she stood up and he took her hand and led her onto the dance floor, leaving some disgruntled women in her wake.
'You look stunning Lori.'
Lori blushed but didn't say anything, for she didn't take compliments well.
Then a shiver went through her when he put his arms around her, and she smiled up at him and said, 'Why did you pick me?'

Pulling her closer to him he whispered, 'Why wouldn't I? You are the best-looking woman in the room.'
She smiled and said no more because she wanted to savour the moment.

'You look beautiful tonight Lori,' he said lovingly, and she looked up at him and said, 'You too.'
He kissed her cheek and pulled her closer, and she felt herself blush. She hoped that when the night ended and they'd slept together, (yes, she was going to sleep with him) he would want to see her again.
If not, she would remember this night forever. She'd found her Prince Charming, even if it was for one night only.

'Mind if I have this dance?' Jane asked.
They stopped dancing and lori went to walk away.
'Where do you think you're going,' Jon said, as he pulled her back. 'I'm sorry Jane, I'm busy, and we'll be dancing together all night.'
With that, Jane walked off in a huff.
'That's if it's alright with you Lori?'
Lori smiled and cuddled into him, hoping, but not expecting, that something would come of this relationship. However, just in case this was it, she intended to make the most of it.

She was no longer looking out of the window hoping that one day she would find her Prince Charming. For tonight at least, she was living the dream. And she knew, if nothing came of this relationship, she would remember this night forever. Hopefully, it would give her the confidence to start dating.

Deception

As Jen walked into the coffee shop, she couldn't help but notice the man looking thoughtfully at his computer screen. He was wearing black trousers and a short sleeved blue shirt and looked as if he'd just stepped out of the office. He must have been about thirty. He had short brown hair, slightly greying at the temples which made him look distinguished. After paying for her latte and biscuits, she walked to the back of the coffee shop, making sure that she could see him; but he couldn't see her.

She wondered what he was doing. Was he looking at work emails, or was he writing an email to his girlfriend? Or was he trawling the internet looking for a date. If he was, he would see her face plastered on most of the dating sites.

She was thirty-five and still a virgin, and she hadn't even had a proper boyfriend, which is why, she was spending most nights on the internet searching for one. That was a lie, she did have a boyfriend many moons ago, but she never mentioned his name, not since he'd cheated on her with several of her friends. Still, like mum always said, *'You have to kiss a lot of frogs before you find your prince.'* Sadly, she couldn't even find a frog.

As the man got up from the chair, Jen watched him walk over to the counter and order another drink. He had a relaxed manner about him and when he stood talking to the Barista, she was a little jealous, because he seemed to be able to hold a conversation. Whereas she, could hardly string a few words together.

She pulled out her laptop and logged into her favourite dating site, 'Love Happens.'
Her favourite site because she'd had at least four people like her. Sadly, three of them looked to be a hundred, and one didn't even have a picture.

She took a sip of her coffee then started to look on the dating sites to see if he was on any of them, and ten minutes later, she spotted him on one. So, unlike her, he didn't appear to be desperate. She decided to read his biography. He was single and the managing director of a large company.

Of course, he was the boss. Why else would he be sitting in a coffee shop at ten to three on a weekday.
Another ten minutes passed, and the man was still sitting there, but this time he was reading a book and eating a sandwich; he certainly had time on his hands.
Disheartened, Jen walked towards the exit and as she went to walk out, the man in question ran over and held the door open for her, and when she looked into his brown eyes, she smiled.

'Hi, I'm Stefan Thomas.'
Startled a little, it took her a little while to answer, but eventually she said, 'Jenny Brown.'
'Pleased to meet you Jenny Brown.'
Then he put his hand gently on the small of her back and led her out of the coffee shop.
'I was wondering if I could take you out to dinner,' he asked, as he smiled down at her.

He was tall, that was a bonus.
'I'd like that, thank you.'

'Would sometime next week be alright? I don't think I've got anything on next week,' he said, as he itched his ear. They exchanged phone numbers and then he said, 'I'm sorry, I've got to go. I may be the boss, but I've spent too long out of the office waiting for you. I'll see you next week.'

She watched him walk away and smiled. He had said he'd been waiting for her, why? She decided she would let that fact slide for now because she needed to get home and delete all her profiles on those dating sites, because she didn't want to appear desperate, which of course she was.

The Date

Two days later Stefan messaged her to ask if she would like to go for dinner with him the following Thursday, and being her dart night, she apologised and said that she couldn't make it, and could they make it another time. Whereupon, he messaged back to say that he could do the Wednesday after, and where would she like him to pick her up. It was agreed, in two weeks' time, he was going to pick her up at eight, outside the coffee shop.

Jenny looked at the dress on the hanger and wondered if she should try it on. It had a low top, which would probably show off some of her ample bosom, and it was short, which would show off her dumpy legs. After five minutes, she'd made up her mind. She was going to wear trousers and a plain black top, which was safe and would show nothing; for she wasn't one for flaunting her assets, of which there were many.

It was ten past eight and she'd been standing across the street from the coffee shop for the last half an hour and there was still no sign of him. She would give him ten minutes then head on home.

Sadly, she was still standing there at nine, and feeling disgusted with herself for waiting for him, half-heartedly, she pulled her mobile phone out of her bag. She searched the screen for the message icon...nothing.

Brushing the tear from her eye, she ran towards the bus stop. If she was quick, she could get the next bus home.
'Hey watch it!'
'Sorry,' she said, as she rubbed the man's arm. 'You're not hurt, are you?'
When she looked up, it was to see Stefan looking down at her and he said, 'Where were you?'
'Where were you?' she said haughtily.
'In the coffee shop, it closes late on a Wednesday. Apparently, it was singles night.'

Frowning, she said, 'Did you meet anyone?'
'We had a date remember?'
'I was waiting over the road, I thought you had stood me up.'
Grabbing hold of her hand, he pulled her along the road and said, 'I've got a great night planned.'
She smiled, he was taking control, and for now, she liked that.

Walking into the car park, they walked over to Stefan's silver Audi and he opened the door for her, and she slid into the passenger seat, and as they drove along the coast road, she looked out across the bay to Portland. Suddenly, even though it was getting dark, everything seemed brighter, more beautiful, clearer, and yes, extraordinary.
'What are you thinking?' he asked.
'I need someone to pinch me, this feels surreal. I'm sitting next to a handsome man, in one of the prettiest places on earth and it feels like a dream.'
He laughed, then realising she was serious he said, 'You don't get out much, do you?'

Now, they were standing by the Olympic Rings on Portland. The sun was going down and the view was breath-taking, and she wanted to cry.
So, what, if she was reading too much into this date. She'd never felt this relaxed in ages and it felt as if she'd known Stefan for ages. She felt comfortable in his company and safe too.
But of course, the bubble had to burst.

'Is that you Stefan? Bloody hell, what brings you this way?' and before he had a chance to answer, the beautiful woman in front of her said, 'Who are you?'
His face flushed red then he said sternly, 'Don't start Chrissy.'
The woman looked at him crossly and said, 'It didn't take you long did it.' Then she turned to Jenny and said sarcastically, 'You want to watch this one. He's got a reputation in this area. He'll get you up the duff and then leave you.'

Jenny blushed and took her hand out of his and sighed. Of course, it had all been too good to be true, well, more fool her.
'Don't take any notice of her. I've only got one son, and there's no guarantee he's even mine, isn't that right,' he said angrily, looking into Chrissy's face, daring her to lie.
'Actually, I don't care. If you don't mind Stefan, the nights gone a bit flat for me, would you take me home?'

Turning into her road, he pulled up outside her mother's house, walked around to her side of the car and opened the door for her. She waited until he'd locked the door, then they walked up the path and when they reached the front door, he kissed her on the cheek and said, 'I'm sorry, any chance we can start again?'
She smiled, 'I don't see why not. Who was that woman?'
'That money grabbing cow is my ex-wife, lovely, isn't she? Sadly, she turned my head and well, the rest is history.'
'What about your son, you weren't exactly kind about him.'
'He's only two months, I'm waiting for the paternity results. I don't want to bond with him, only to find out that he's not mine.'
'Some might think you are being callous.'
'Are you one of them?'
'Honestly, I don't know.'
'I can understand where you are coming from. I'm sorry you feel like that. Perhaps we should nail this on the head until I'm more settled.'
Biting back a tear, she nodded.
He kissed her on the cheek and left and suddenly, she felt terrible, because she'd taken what the woman had said at face value and hadn't given him a chance. She would ring him in a couple of days.

'Hi,' Jenny whispered.

'Hey.'

'I'm sorry our date ended the way it did. I'd like to make it up to you.'

He smiled and said, 'That's great, fancy a coffee in our favourite coffee shop?'

'Yes, I'd like that.'

That's if you're not working of course, I don't know what you do for a living. In fact, I don't really know that much about you. We'll soon remedy that though, three o'clock tomorrow afternoon alright with you?'

'Thankfully, tomorrow is my day off, I'll see you there.'

Stefan put the phone down and picked the two envelopes up, opened them and smiled. He was no longer married, and the baby wasn't his. He didn't mean to be so callous, but he didn't really want to be a part time dad. When he had his family, he would be a hands-on father.

Jenny had butterflies in her stomach as she turned on the computer. She liked Stefan, and it was obvious he liked her; now she had to Google him to see if he was the person, she hoped he was. After all, he wasn't just attractive, he owned his own company and had his own home.

He was boyfriend material for sure, but then she'd thought her ex was, only to find out that he'd lied about everything. He hadn't worked in a garage, he lived with his mates and he wasn't working. She wouldn't have minded that, but he'd slept with everything in a skirt and she wasn't having that. She knew that he wasn't getting it from her, but he could have waited...if he'd loved her enough.

First, she looked at the dating sites and he was only on one of them, which she already knew. Then, she typed in his name and found out that he was divorcing his wife on the grounds of adultery and that his wife was pregnant. There were pictures of him and his wife together and they looked happy.

His wife was stunning, so much better looking than she was. He was thirty- five and loved walking and reading when he had time. Nothing too stressful or worrying there then, unlike her ex who was into skateboarding and motor track racing which she'd funded; more fool her.

She felt reassured, after all, she had to make sure he was the real deal. She didn't want to get to know him, only to find he wasn't the right one. After all, she only had his dating site picture to go by and Luke could have been having her on.

Jenny walked into the café and when Stefan saw her, he stood up and walked over to her. He shook her hand and she sat opposite him, and he walked to the counter and came back three minutes later with two coffees and some wafer biscuits and sat down.
'I'm glad you came, I must have seemed a bit heartless the other day, I didn't mean to be, I was just stating the truth.'
'I like that in a man. I'm sorry to say, that I was too quick to judge.'
'Still, I'd like to make it up to you. Would you like to come to Cornwall with me on Christmas Eve? I've booked a lovely cottage down there for a few days, we might as well use it.'
'I'd love too, thanks.'
'Good, now drink up and we'll start packing.'

'I love a man who takes control,' she said, trying to flirt with him.

As Stefan led her out of the café he smiled, his plan was working. He was pleased with his choice. She worked in one of the shops he owned, and his manager had told him that she was a virgin and would make a good mother. When he'd googled all those dating websites, he'd realised that she was easy pickings. He'd been right, that first day in the café, he had her eating out of his hand.

She wasn't particularly good- looking but she had a good personality; what he'd seen of it. She was perfect. He'd wanted to start a family for so long and being a little self-conscious and not comfortable with herself, he would be able to mould her into the perfect mother, unlike his unfaithful ex-wife. The fact that Jenny was a virgin was a bonus. Besides, arranged marriages happened every day, so he wasn't really hoodwinking her. Marrying for love hadn't worked out, so why not try this way.

As they walked along the street, Jen looked up at Stefan and smiled, and he kissed her on the cheek. Then she looked ahead as they avoided the people walking towards them. She was sure she'd picked the right man. He was rich, had his own business and owned his own home. He was everything she needed in a man. He would make a great father.

She had wanted a family for ages and time was running out for her, and she was having to take drastic action. After talking to her best friend, Luke, the manager of the store where she worked, he'd mentioned that Stefan was looking for a wife and from that day on, she'd set about getting him; and once Luke had mentioned her to Stefan, it was game on.

Luckily, after googling him, she'd decided that he was the perfect man. His personality was ok, and the fact that his web site said that he owned a large company and wanted to start a family, was in his favour. Hopefully, they would grow fond of each other, if not, when their children had grown up, she would move on. Preferably, with some money she'd stashed away over the years.

When Jen snuggled into him, Stefan stopped walking, turned to her and said, 'What do you think about having children?'
Not wanting to give the game away, she said coyly, 'I'd love a family, times ticking, as they say.' They both laughed and Stefan put his arm around her, and both feeling smug, they walked into town.

As people passed by, and looked at this happy smiling couple, nobody would have suspected the deceit that lay behind their happy demeanour and smiling faces.

A Soldier's Pledge.
(Historical)

Selena put down the soap and scrubbing brush and wiped the sweat from her forehead, and for a second, she wondered why on earth she had volunteered to be a nurse at St Mary's. Being a recruit, she'd been on cleaning and bedpan duty for over a month now and hadn't done any real nursing.

'Miss Shaw, you are needed in ward two,' matron said bombastically.
Silently, Selena walked by her, careful not to look at the ogre, who was carefully disguised as a woman.

'Hold the bloody man still while I take his leg,' the surgeon yelled, and she ran over to the table and held the man's hand.'
The surgeon looked at her and said sarcastically, 'Are you stupid. Hold his ankle down.'
Selena walked to the end of the table; somebody was holding down his good leg and she put both hands on his foot and shuddered.
'This is the third one this week,' the surgeon grumbled, as he held the mask over the man's face.

Selena bit her lip when the man began to struggle and she climbed on top of the table to keep his ankle down, and the man next to her did the same. Then tears streamed down her face as she watched the patient writhe in pain, as the surgeon hacked at his leg. It was a blunt saw and she flinched every time the blade got stuck in the bone. Surely, somebody could invent something to make this process less harrowing.

As Selena washed her hands, the man who had been helping walked over to her, put his hands under the tap and whispered, 'You won't last long if you are going to act like that. I know it's your first time, but don't show them you have feelings because they will see that as a sign of weakness, and you'll be out on your ear.

Selena looked at him, frowned, but didn't say anything because she knew he was right. She would have to try and be less vocal in future.

It had been over a week now and Matron hadn't called her into the office, and she was grateful that nobody had reported her. However, the surgeon hadn't asked for her again and she was still scrubbing everything in sight. When she'd told the head of the workhouse that she was interested in nursing, she hadn't realised it would be so boring. Still, she was grateful for them for finding her a position. At least she didn't have to go into service like some of her friends.

The dormitory, her home for now, was minimalistic but clean and she'd made some friends. Granted, she rarely saw them, because their one day off a week didn't coincide with hers, but they were still friends and when they were working together, they had some laughs; when that cow Miss Carter wasn't around.

Then suddenly, all the staff were called into the lecture hall and as they sat waiting for the professors, she could hear people muttering. Like her, many hoped to see an autopsy being performed on a real cadaver, and others talked about their loved ones going to war. Also, someone was putting it around that they were looking for nurses to go to Constantinople.

As the Doctors, Surgeons and Professors walked in, a deathly hush went around the room and the students stood up.
'Sit down please, Doctor Brown has an announcement.'

Mr Brown stood up, ran his hands through his grey hair, pulled out his notebook, cleared his throat, opened the notebook, closed it again and then put it back in his pocket.

Clearing his throat again, then looking straight at her he said, 'As you know, we are at war with Russia, a sad situation indeed. I'll get to the point. Florence Nightingale has been asked to put a team of nurses together to go there and care for our brave men on the front line. I have here a list of names that have been put forward by your mentors. When I read them out, you will come to the front.

Knowing that her name would not be called, and not sure if she wanted to go anyway, she was just about to walk out when she heard her name, and along with several others she walked to the front of the room and looked at the strangers in front of her. She was the only one from her dormitory to be picked and was disappointed that none of her friends were going.

'Everyone return to your duties, and you lot,' he said, pointing to her and the others, 'Stay here. You are going to be debriefed.'

It was settled, they were sailing tomorrow, along with Miss Nightingale. So, 1854 was proving to be an eventful year after all, but whether it was going to be a good year was a different matter.

While they were being debriefed, several people tried to decline the offer, but when it came down to it, they had very little to say on the matter and had to go whether they liked it or not. Selena wasn't sure if they had picked them because they were good at their job, or because they weren't. Either way, none of them were looking forward to the experience.

Filth

When they arrived at the hospital Selena couldn't believe what she was seeing. Bodies were lying on the floor in the hallways whilst rats and bugs ran over them; and some were lying in their own filth. The wards were just as filthy as the hallways and half of the men seemed to be malnourished. When she asked for a glass of water for a patient, she was told that it was on ration.

Suddenly, the idea of being a nurse wasn't so appealing after all, and when she retired to the filth ridden dormitory that was to be her home for the foreseeable future, she sat on her bed and cried, and she wasn't the only one. As she listened in the darkness, she could hear others sobbing.

Two days later when she walked into the hospital with a group of nurses, Miss Nightingale gave them a scrubbing brush and some soap and they set about cleaning the hospital, while the doctors and Miss Nightingale dealt with the patients. Some had to be taken into sterile wards and quarantined because there was an epidemic of cholera and typhoid. Thankfully, a few days later, fresh linen arrived and within three weeks, the place was clean.

Miss Nightingale had also set up a kitchen which prepared healthy meals for the men, and a laundry, with its own workforce; which enabled the nurses to get on with the business of saving lives. St Mary's was clean, but this place was spotless and over the next few months, the death rate declined and Selena, not being terribly adept at being a nurse, had been sent to the classroom to help. Sadly, although she pulled her weight, she'd had to accept that she wasn't cut out for nursing, what with her nearly fainting every time she saw blood or had to clean a wound.

Thankfully, a school room had been set up to broaden the minds of the patients and to give them something to do, and noticing that she was good with numbers and words, the doctors had given her the position of teacher. In the end, she was given the job permanently, for which she was eternally grateful.

Although she had some patients interested in learning, she tended to do art a lot, or go on nature walks, which is where she'd met her beloved.

She'd been walking home one night after finishing her shift when she'd seen a young man, slightly inebriated, staggering towards her. At first, she was a little unnerved by the sight of him and wondered whether she should go back to the hospital. However, just when she was about to turn around, he'd said, 'Hi, I'm lost.'
'Where are you going,' she'd asked.
It turned out that he was a 'walking wounded' and she showed him to ward 6. He was lucky, four more weeks and he would be released. As she'd walked out the door, he'd asked for a date, and as she was attracted to him, she'd said yes, and tonight they were going to a party in the men's dormitory.

Selena and her friends had taken to wearing black dresses as a sign of respect for the fallen and injured, and although she desperately wanted to wear something bright, she stuck to her black dress.

'What's with the black dresses?' Jonah asked thoughtfully, as he pointed to the ladies.
'It's a sign of respect, none of us feel like celebrating when so many young men lay dead or dying.'
'Oh, I see. I'm glad you decided to come here tonight.'
'I had nothing else to do.'
His eyes smiling, he said cheekily, 'That's a lie Selena Taylor, because I know you changed your day off to come here tonight. Your friend Rosa told me. She's seeing my mate Luke.'
'No need to get big headed. A girl likes to get out occasionally, there's nothing wrong with that, is there?'
'Blimey girl, who's got your back up?'
'Sorry, I just don't want you to get the wrong idea about me. I'm not easy.'
'I never said you was, mores the pity. Do you want to go back to your dormitory?'
'I'll stay a while, it's just that, I want to put this out there. I find you attractive and if I go with you, there's no knowing what I'd get up to and we both know, that can't happen. These are terrible times.'
'I know,' he whispered.'

She wrapped her arms around him, and he kissed her forehead, and she was certain now that they had an understanding, even though she'd only known him for a few hours. She couldn't believe how she was being so friendly and forward, but she was smitten with him.

Over the next two weeks, they saw each other as often as they could, but it wasn't enough, and Selena would cry herself to sleep most nights because she missed him so much, and when he saw her, he would tell her the same.

There was no knowing how long their romance would last, but there was no getting away from the fact that they loved each other. To the point that she wanted to sleep with him and would have done if he'd made the first move; but he was too much of a gentleman to do that. Which of course was the right thing to do, especially if she fell pregnant and he died. It was a harsh thing to have to come to terms with, but it was a fact of life now.

Then, two weeks later, that dreadful day arrived when he was to be released. He was going back to the front, and even though he said everything would be alright, judging by the soldiers that came to the hospital, she knew, his chances weren't good.

Her face wet with tears, Selena looked up at him and said, 'Promise you'll write to me whenever you can.'
'Don't worry, take this, I've written my address on the envelope, give me yours and we'll write to each other and I swear, I will come back to you. I swear it.'
Trying to hold back the tears, Selena said, 'Don't make any promises,' and then she wrote her address down and he put it in his pocket, knowing full well that surviving this war was going to be difficult.
'Take this,' he said, handing her a gold locket.

She took it from him and opened it. Inside was a picture of a beautiful lady and she looked at him and frowned.
'That's my mother and there's a lock of hair behind the picture, she said it would bring me good luck, I want you to have it.'

Selena went to hand it back, but he would not take it and she said angrily, 'Your mother gave you this.'

'My mother would want you to have it,' he said, closing her open hand and then kissing her knuckles. It was then that Selena broke down. She had finally met the man of her dreams and she was going to lose him to a war that nobody wanted.

He held her tightly for a little while, then gently kissed her on the lips, pushed her gently away from him and said, 'Return the locket to me when I return.'

She sniffed back a tear as she watched him march away, hoping he would look back at her, but he didn't.

Hell

1855 and Jonah was in the thick of it and life was hell. He hadn't seen Selena for what seemed like for ever and if it wasn't for her image in his mind, he would have succumbed to the cold weeks ago.

Rations were short; they had no winter clothes or tents; no medical supplies; and they were eating meat without cooking it, because there was no fuel. Soldiers were dying daily and there was nothing any of them could do about it.

'I'm so cold,' a young lad sitting next to him said, and Jonah wrapped his blanket around him. The lad was grateful, and when he started to sob, Jonah held him tightly. He couldn't have been any older than sixteen and the lad started to call for his mother. Then unexpectedly, he jumped up and went to run over the trench, but a soldier managed to grab him, and he was taken away.

Later that day, they found him on the battlefield, he'd been run through.

Life for Selena was getting worse; the wounded were coming in droves and she'd had to go back to nursing, and it was heart-breaking. Soldiers were dying while they waited to be seen, and she was horrified when she saw surgeons marking their foreheads with letters, trying to work out who could be saved. To make matters worse, the number of amputees was growing, and she had to resume her old position and restrain the patients.

The hospital was starting to run out of food, water, and medical supplies, and she wondered how long it would be before they'd no longer be able to help the patients. She dreaded that day with a vengeance.

Soldiers were no longer being buried and were placed in the woods, ready for burial when things got better. But it had been weeks now and the patients were increasing, and their facilities were at breaking point.

Her life was made worse by the fact that she'd only received one letter from Jonah in six months and she wasn't sure if he was alive or dead. And every time a soldier came in who looked vaguely like him, her heart would beat faster.

Finally, 1856 and the war was over, but still the wounded kept on coming and Selena felt as if she was going mad. All the nurses were tired and overworked and she was living in a kind of bubble and couldn't escape from it. Until some new recruits came and finally, all the staff were able to get some much-earned sleep. After she'd retired to bed, she didn't get up for three days. She just couldn't muster herself, but had too, when she heard her friend's voice.

'Get up Selena, we have work to do.'
Looking at Rosa through blurry eyes, she said, 'Oh Rosa, let me be.'
'Luke needs to talk to you, it's about Jonah.'
Selena stood up immediately, got dressed then followed her friend to the dormitories, then stood by a window in the office, preparing herself for the worst.

When Luke walked into the office, Selena put her hand over her mouth and gasped, Rosa was trying her best to hold Luke up. Despondently, Rosa looked at Selena, shook her head and quickly wiped away the tears.

Luke had a bandage around his head and Selena could see that he'd been shot in the head. Rosa was trying to be brave but was failing miserably.
Rosa squeezed his arm and sat down, and he said, 'I must look a bloody sight, I'm sorry I can't see you. At least I'm walking, at least for a while. The surgeon says I still have shrapnel in my head, and he doesn't know how long I'll last. Rosa is standing by me, but to tell you the truth, I'll be happy to leave this god forsaken world.'
Rosa started to cry, and he put his arm around her and said bravely, 'Don't take on so. I don't want to be a burden to you, I know I'm not long for this world, these headaches tell me that. Anyway, I've got some letters from Jonah.'

Selena reached out for the blood-soaked letters and put them in her pocket, and trying not to sound troubled she said, 'What of Jonah?'

'I'm afraid I don't know, we got separated while we were being transported here. I heard some canons and the next thing I knew, our wagon overturned, and I heard screaming. Hopefully, he got out, but he should have been here by now. I wish it was better news.'

'It was good of you to give me the letters, thank you.'

'We'd better get you back on the ward, the surgeon said you were to take it easy remember?'

'I'm sorry Rosa, but sod the surgeon, I'm off to get some rum. If I'm going to die, I'm not going to wait around until it happens. Are you coming?'

'I've got to go. See you soon Selena. I'm on duty tonight, if anybody else is brought in, I'll let you know.'

Rosa rolled her eyes, then with despair written all over her face, she looked at Selena and then reached out for Luke's hand. If the shot didn't get him, the rum would.

When Selena got to the dormitory, she placed the letters in a suitcase and went back to work. She didn't want to read them just yet, for she was sure they were filled with dreadful things. She would read them when she got back home.

The Waiting Game

It had been over nine months now and there had been no news of Jonah, and Selena had learnt to accept that he was probably dead. As for Luke, he was still alive, although Rosa had written to say that he was in a wheelchair now and could no longer walk. She had returned to England with him and they were living with his parents. Reading between the lines, Rosa wasn't happy, but felt obliged to stay with him.

Selena packed her bag, and along with some other nurses she set sail for England, back to a school in Dorset where she'd found work as a teacher in a little rural town she'd never heard of. Surprisingly, she'd received a letter from a Mrs Petty, offering her a position.

'It is so good to see you my dear, we've been without a teacher for such a long time. You have your own little place attached to the school, it's not much, but it will do for one. I've put the essentials in there, so you won't need to go into town for a while.'
'That's kind of you Mrs Petty, but please excuse me, I really do have to send a letter today, it is most urgent.'
'No worries, I will give it to the courier when I go that way.'
'Thank you, it's a letter to the orphanage. I need them to direct my letters here.'
'Expecting mail, are we?'
'Sadly no, but you never know. If you'll excuse me, I'll make my way to the school.'
'My house is only down the road so I will expect you for Sunday dinner, about twelve suit you?'
'Yes, thank you miss…'
'The names Lil dear, we don't stand on formalities here.'
'Thank you, Lil.'

When Selena walked into the school room, she couldn't believe how well stocked it was. It had chalk and slates for everyone and stacks of exercise books and pencils. Mrs Petty had placed green ferns around the room, and it looked welcoming.

The house alongside it was similar, it consisted of one room, but it had an open fire where she could cook. It also had a bed and a small outhouse, and she liked it.

A week to go before Christmas and the snow was starting to settle, and she knew that she wouldn't be seeing any children for some weeks, but still, it would give her time to make a plan of action, for she had no idea where to begin. They wouldn't only need art, they needed to learn their numbers and writing. Suddenly, there was a knock at the door which made her jump. Armed with a poker, she slowly opened the door.

'Hello, I'm Mr Smart, caretaker on this estate. Mrs Petty asked me to drop by to see if you needed anything?'
'Oh yes, she told me you might come by, would you like a drink.'
'No thanks, I best be getting home, the wife will be waiting to cook this lot,' he said happily, as he pointed to the birds and squirrels hanging from a pole.'
She screwed her face up and said, 'Well done.'
'This is nothing, you wait until Spring, they'll be lots of beasts around. I'll bring you some when the weather turns.'
'I would be most grateful, thank you Mr Smart.'
'Well, better get going, before we all get snowed in. Are you sure you don't need anything?'
'I'm ok thank you; Mrs Petty has stocked the kitchen and I brought some things too.'
Satisfied that she would be alright for the winter, he said his goodbyes and she watched him walk up the hill.

Although it was Sunday and she was due to go to Mrs Petty's for dinner, she decided to stay home. She didn't know the place well enough to go venturing out in the snow. There could be all sorts of dangers on the way, traps, holes, or even wild animals.

At ten to one, somebody banged on the door. For such a rural place, she'd been inundated with visitors today, who was it this time?'
'Hello, miss, how are you?'
'Very well thank you,' she said opening the door a little.
He laughed and said, 'You've nothing to fear from me miss, I'm way beyond my prime. I'm Mr Fletcher. I make arrows for hunting with, and I work for Lord Broxley who owns all the land around here.'
'Pleased to meet you.'
Mr Fletcher took of his cap and said, 'Likewise, is there anything you need?'
'No thank you but thank you for asking. Please excuse me, I've got some hot milk on the fire.'
'Surely. I live ten minutes away if you need anything, or just want to chatter. I live with my wife in a little cottage down the road.'
'That's very kind of you, thank you.'
Then she waved him off and gently closed the door behind her, wrapped her blanket around her and walked over to the fire.

Once she'd warmed herself, she took Jonah's letters out of the suitcase, got into bed, and opened the first one. She could see that Jonah was jovial when he had written the letter and he was looking forward to seeing her again. In the next letter he talked off his love for her and she smiled. Although they had only known each other a short while, she loved him too.

Sadly, the following letters were full of hatred for their enemies and he was also moaning about the government, who he said were leaving them out there to die. She didn't read any more, they would only bring back memories of things she'd rather forget, as it was, she woke up several times a week sweating and screaming because she still dreamt about her time at the hospital.

The following two months went by so slowly that she thought she would die of boredom. Plus, she had hoped that Jonah had survived the war and doing so, would have made his way to her door, but it didn't look likely now.

She'd dreamt about him a few times, but after a while, she stopped hoping and now believed him to be dead. She'd cried for a few days and then just accepted her lot, and when the snow melted, she looked forward to her first pupil and sure enough, two days after the thaw, Mr Smart brought the children to school in his wagon.

'Good morning miss, how are you?'
'Very well thank you, but I'm pleased to see a happy face. Do you bring the children to school every day?'
'No miss, only in the Winter. They usually walk here, or their parents bring them.'
'That is kind of you, would you like to come in for a hot drink?'
'No thank you. I've got work to do up at the manor. Oh yes, I nearly forgot, Mrs Petty said she'd love to see you one afternoon for tea. Any day will do her.'
'Tell her I'd love that and will call on her on Wednesday.'
'Will do, I'll be back to pick them up at two. Ten to two is the normal schedule.'
'That is fine with me, see you later.'
Then she called the children into the school room and asked them to read for a bit which they did.

Half an hour later and they were all reciting their two times table and as they did so, she looked around the classroom. She had ten pupils, three boys and seven girls and three of the children were from the same family.
'When can we go out to play Miss?' a young girl asked, and she replied, 'When I say so.' Then she smiled and said, 'Lunch will be at twelve until twelve twenty and you'll get a piece of fruit to take home with you. Mrs Petty has left you some.'
'Mr Drake left us after a week, will you be staying with us?' a boy asked cautiously.
'I hope so, but we don't know what will happen in the future. Now then, as it's your first day back, you may go out to play.'
With that, cheering as they went, the children went out to play and she watched them through the window.

The week went well and at the end of the week, after she'd tested them, she felt pleased with herself. They had got all their spellings and times tables correct. At least they had learnt something.

The following months flew by and before she knew it, it was June and her class had expanded to fifteen. Luckily, they were able to sit outside and learn, because sadly, they only had twelve chairs indoors. She would ask Mr Smart if he could get some more when he called again.

Life was starting to get a little easier for her. She still thought about Jonah, but she'd stopped dreaming about him, and her nightmares were abating. The only thing that troubled her, was the isolation and lack of intelligent adult company.

She'd been to Mrs Petty's cottage a couple of times a week, but the conversation was very dull. She mainly talked about her grown up family and what they were doing up at the manor. Selena longed for some decent conversation.

Luckily, one afternoon when taking tea with Mrs Petty, her nephew and his wife came to stay, and she enjoyed their company. They were down for the summer and Frances and Hugh would often visit her at the school, and they would take walks together, play cards and swim in the lake by the Manor, and she enjoyed the summer immensely.

However, they left at the beginning of September and when November came, she was left alone and had closed the school for the next four months; for the parents were reluctant to bring the children out in Winter. She tried to fill her time with reading and writing but some days, she was bored out of her mind and wondered how long it would be before she looked for another position. That, or get away for a few months to stem the boredom.

In her letters, Rosa had said that she could go and stay with her whenever she wanted, and Selena knew that she could do with the help. Poor Luke was bedbound now and Rosa wasn't sure how much she could take.

Selena took the small box from under the bed and counted out the coins. She had more than enough for the journey and her mind was set. She would walk into town and get passage on the next wagon and spend a week or so with her best friend. Two days later, she was on her way to the seaside.

A Welcome Break

When she arrived at Luke and Rosa's house, she was a little disappointed, it looked like a hovel, and she wondered where on earth she would sleep. Perhaps she should have told her she was coming.
'Good grief Selena, is that you?' Rosa said, pleased to see her friend.
'I'm sorry I didn't send word, only, I thought I'd be welcome.'
'You are, you are. I am so glad you are here. How long will you stay?'
'I thought a month might do it, or less if you like.'
'A month it is. My, teaching certainly agrees with you, come in.'

As Selena walked into the hovel, she was surprised to see that it was spotless.
'You can sleep in here if that's alright. I've got plenty of blankets.' Then, she cuddled Selena tightly, for it was so good to see her friend.
'Come and say hello to Luke, but don't be surprised if he doesn't recognise you, he's slipping away from us minute by minute, and to tell it as it is, I love the man, but I'm not sure how long I'll be able to put up with this,' she said angrily.
'I'm so sorry, let me look after him for a while, go out and have some fun.'
'Perhaps in a couple of days, that will be nice. Now, whatever you do, don't cry when you see him.'

Selena followed her into the bedroom and remembering what Rosa had said, she looked down at him and smiled.

However, the place smelt like rotting flesh and Luke was just skin and bones. He tried to raise his hand when she said hello but couldn't.
'It's good to see you Luke.'
He tried to smile as she kissed him on the cheek but couldn't quite manage it.
'Selena is staying with us for a couple of weeks my love, isn't that great?'
Again, he did not move and when he tried to say something, he couldn't, and a solitary tear ran down his face.

Later that evening, sitting by the fire, Rosa started to cry, and Selena held her tightly, and when she was strong enough to speak Rosa said, 'I don't know what to do. The surgeon said there's nothing they can do for him, and I can't write to his parents, they think he's dead. Luke wanted it that way.'
'I can help for a bit.'
'You can't, he won't let anyone touch him except me.'
'I'm so sorry Rosa, how can I help?'
'When he's asleep, you can watch over him while I go and see my mother, I haven't seen her for ages.'
'Certainly.'

Later that night, as Rosa walked to her mothers, a drunken thug stepped in front of her and in a case of mistaken identity, he put an axe in her head, and when the police came round to tell Selena, she cried for a while, then wondered how the hell she was going to tell Luke.

However, when she swished the curtain open, it was to see him lying dead on the floor and she fell to her knees and sobbed. Not for Luke who she barely knew, but for

Rosa, whose kindness to others had been rewarded with a blow to the head.

A week later, and she watched them bury them in a pauper's grave at the back of the church and a day later, she left the hovel and got the wagon home, much to the relief of Mrs Petty who'd thought she'd deserted them.

'Where have you been? We were worried sick about you.'
'My friend and her husband died, (she wasn't going to tell her that they weren't married) and I had to go to the funeral.
'Oh dear, I am so sorry. But you're not planning on leaving us, are you?'
'No Mrs Petty,' she said reluctantly. Then added, 'Get yourself settled. I'll make us some tea.'
'I've brought a fruit cake,' Lil said, sensing an air of hostility.
'That will be very welcome, thank you Lil. Excuse me whilst I get out of these wet clothes.'
'Certainly, I'll pour the tea. I've also come with a message from Lord Broxley, he wants to talk with you. He's sending a horse for you the day after tomorrow, is that alright?'
Selena smiled to herself, finally, something was going to happen.
'That's fine, did he say what time?'
'About 4, I think.'

Two days later, the horse and cart pulled up outside the schoolhouse and she pulled the blanket around her and walked out to it.
'Are you Miss Taylor?'

Selena nodded and got up onto the cart and sat next to the man, and they sat in silence all the way to the manor, which thankfully, was only a ten -minute ride away.

As they pulled up outside the manor, Selena gasped with excitement; the house was enormous. She followed the man into the great hall and sat down on one of the benches and the man left the room.

Ten minutes later, Lord Broxley made an appearance and she smiled, he looked a bit like Jonah. He had dark brown hair and a beard, and his blue eyes looked the same as Jonah's.
'It is good to see you Selena, welcome to Broxley manor. We have heard a lot about you, my son Jonah often spoke of you in his letters.'
A tear fell from the corner of her eye and she said shyly, 'You are Jonah's father, is he alive?'
'We don't know, I have people looking for him but so far, nothing. Somebody saw him fall from the ambulance and walk away, but nothing since. I don't suppose you know where he is?'
'No, I miss him.'

'Still, we have hope, do we not. The main reason I want to see you, is because my daughter goes to your school and she thinks you are a wonderful teacher, and I feel uneasy with you living out there. If my son was to come home, he would not thank me for leaving you alone in the countryside like that, and I don't want that. I've turned one of the rooms at the far end of the house into a school room and you can stay in Jonah's room.'

'It is a very good offer, but I am not in need of charity. I already have a home and schoolroom. I feel I must decline your offer, for you owe me nothing. I loved your son, but we only knew each other a few weeks. I fear living here will bring back painful memories for me and I'd rather stay where I am.'
'Very well, but the offer will always be there.'
'If you wouldn't mind, I'd like to get home before it gets dark. However, if you have any news concerning Jonah, please let me know. Your son was a kind and generous soul and I miss him terribly.'
'I will do that, Smart, take Miss Selena home.'

The Return

Selena was decorating the room when there was a knock at the door. Startled, Selena took the poker from the fire and raised it in the air and walked to the door.
'Whoever you are, I've got a weapon and I'm prepared to use it.'
'It's me, Mr Fletcher, I've some news from the manor.'
She dropped the poker and unlocked the door and said, 'What news have you?'
'Can I come in; it's freezing out here.'

He walked to the fire and then turned to her and said, 'Master Broxley has been seen in France.'
She fell onto the seat by the fire and looked into the distance. She was shocked. After all this time, could he still be alive?'
'We got the message a week ago and the master has gone over there in case it's true. He told me to come and give you the news. Now, if you are alright, I better get home.'
'Thank you for telling me Mr Fletcher.'

'You're welcome,' he said, as he walked out the door, still shivering from the cold.

Having locked the door and lit several candles, she was now sat in bed thinking about what Mr Fletcher had said. He had been spotted in France, how could that be?'
She was excited and scared at the same time. She wasn't sure if she still had feelings for him. What if he came home injured like Luke? Would she have enough courage to stay with him. Would he still like her? Would that spark be there? After all, she'd known him for less than a month.

A few days later and she received a message from the manor. Jonah was home and was asking after her, and would she kindly visit them as soon as possible.
Putting the letter on the table and wrapping her shawl around her, she sat down by the fire. She hadn't known Jonah for long and common sense told her, that any love they'd had in the past, had been down to necessity. He'd been going to war and had needed something to hold on to and that came in the form of her letters, and she in turn had needed something to look forward too.

They had only known each other for a short time, and that wasn't long enough to really know if they loved each other, was it? Still, no matter what she thought about it, she would still go to the manor; she owed him that much.

Stepping down from the carriage, Selena looked up to see a man looking down at her from the attic window and she guessed it was probably Jonah, and suddenly, she felt scared and was in two minds whether to step inside, but it was too late. His father had run down the stairs and was now escorting her into the hall, and she watched as a lone figure started to walk down the stairs.

She knew instantly that it was Jonah and her heart started to beat wildly and beads of sweat appeared on her nose and forehead. She watched as he grabbed hold of the banister and hobbled down the stairs. Something was wrong, and she had to steady herself before he got to the bottom of the stairs.

On the outside, apart from a slight limp, he looked relatively unscathed and she smiled, and he smiled back.
'It's good to see you,' he mumbled, and she hugged him and kissed him on the cheek and stepped back.
'It's been awhile, how are you?' he whispered, as a solitary tear ran down his face.
'Good, you?'
'Mentally, I'm having flashbacks and I can't sleep, and I go through bouts of depression. Physically, I have a gammy leg but nothing serious. I'm not exactly the man I was. I'm sorry, can we speak privately?'

He showed her into the morning room and she sat on a chair by the fire and he stood by the window for a few minutes then said, ' If it wasn't for the memory of you, I don't know if I would have survived the war.'
Looking over to him she smiled and said, 'Looking forward to seeing you helped me to survive too.'
'That's good of you to say that.' Then he walked over to her and said, 'We need to face facts, we are strangers.'
'I know, but we had something really special once. If we take things slowly, perhaps those feelings will come back to us. I know you to be a good person Jonah and that is a fine start.'

'I am not the person I was, I have seen and done some terrible things that I have yet to come to terms with.' Afraid he was going to reject her without giving it a try she said, 'Look, we had something special once and we may be able to have that again. I don't know, but we could at least be friends. Please don't decide yet. I'm going to leave you now. If I hear from you again it will be good, but if not, thank you for some wonderful times and I wish you all the best for the future. Then she took his hand in hers, kissed him on the lips and walked away, and as she did so, she bit her lip, because she knew that she was still attracted to him.

She was warming herself by the fire when there was a knock at the door. It was a young lad with a message from the Manor. She'd been invited for dinner and they were going to send a horse for her at seven o'clock. She invited the boy in because he was freezing to death and gave him some hot milk and some bread, and when he was fully fit, and she'd given him another warm jumper, she allowed him to go.

She had a lot of thinking to do. Should she go to dinner, or get on with her life and move on? Which meant, moving somewhere new because although she loved her job, she couldn't stand the cold dark lonely winters. She was lonely and bored out of her mind. Plus, when she'd seen Jonah, he'd only been civil towards her and she wanted more than that, a lot more. She wanted a proper home, children, and most of all, she wanted her husband to love her as she did him.

Another half an hour and they would be sending someone to pick her up, and she still wasn't sure what she wanted to do. However, she was erring towards going to the manor, because if Jonah had invited her for dinner, surely, he felt something for her. Or was the invitation from his father?

Selena packed what little she had in her suitcase, then waited patiently as time slowly ticked by. When the man eventually came for her, she was going to ask him to take her to Mrs Petty's house where she would stay the night, and then she would go back to the orphanage and teach.

They had sent her a letter a while back asking her to return, but she had hope then, and had put the letter away, but had found it a few weeks ago. Hopefully, the position was still open. Either way, she knew the orphanage would let her stay until she found a new position.

Wrapping her shawl tightly around her and putting on her bonnet, she waited by the window and in the distance, she could see the figure of a man walking towards the hut and as hard as she squinted, she couldn't make out who it was, so she waited patiently for the figure to get to her.

Slowly, she opened the door, and came face to face with Jonah's father and worried, she let him in.
'I'm afraid Jonah has changed his mind, there will be no dinner tonight, he has locked himself in his room and refuses to see anyone.
Disheartened, Selena set about making some hot milk.
'Are you leaving us Selena?' Jonah's father asked, as he looked at the suitcase in the corner of the room.
'Yes, I think it's for the best.'
'You are giving up on my son?'

Selena sat down and sighed, then looking at him said, 'He's given up on me I'm afraid, but that's alright, our love kept us alive, now it's time for us to move on. Besides, we don't really know each other that well.'
'I know he still loves you.'
'It's nice of you to say that, but we both know that it's over between us. Would you do me a favour?' He nodded. 'Would you give him this for me, I was looking after it for him, but it's served its purpose and he should have it back.'

He took the locket of her and said shyly, 'My wife was a great woman, she died a month before Jonah went to war, he must have loved you a great deal to give you that.'
'I know he loved me then, he may even like me now. I'm just glad he came home. Thank you for stopping by, would you mind giving me a lift to Mrs Petty's, I am staying there tonight and moving on tomorrow.'
'Of course not, I'm sorry it didn't work out Selena.'
'Me too. Please tell him I wish him all the luck in the future.'

Jonah looked at the locket, walked over to the table and picked it up. He caressed the front of the locket and whispered, 'I Love you mother,' and then opened it to see a picture of Selena's face looking up at him, and he snapped the locket shut. He sighed, then he lay on his bed and sobbed; he was a broken man. He was plagued with dark thoughts and violent dreams and had done and seen some terrible things that he could not come to terms with. He had a lot of healing to do before he could love Selena like he should.

He loved her, there was no doubt in his mind about that, but he had demons to fight and he wouldn't put her through that. It was right that he ended it now, to save Selena from a lot of heartache in the future. This was the best way; he was sure of it.

Time to Go
(A Ghost Story)

Looking at the presents on the table, Rebecca wondered if she should open them now, or leave them until this evening. In the end, she decided to leave them, after all, she'd bought them and wrapped them herself, so there were no surprises there.

Who would have thought that at thirty- eight, she would be unmarried and childless? Still, she had her cat Benji if she needed a cuddle. Then she looked around the flat and noticed that he was nowhere to be seen. That was typical of him, he was never there when you needed him.

'Are you there,' she heard Mrs Smith scream down the hall.
'No, I've gone for a walk,' Rebecca shouted back, as she opened the door.
'Then Mrs Smith barged into the room and sat on the sofa, put the cat on her knee and started to stroke it. She had a terrible habit of coming and going when she felt like it.
'I'm sorry Mrs Smith, I'm going out. Please excuse me.
Mrs Smith smiled up at her, at least she thought she had, because with her roving glass eye, there was really no way of knowing.

'I'm going Mrs Smith,' she said, pointing to the door and when she didn't move, Rebecca said, 'Ok, just make sure you lock up when you leave.'
Rebecca was angry with herself now. She knew she should be more severe with her, even report her to the landlord, but she felt sorry for the poor old dear.

As Rebecca walked towards the door, she looked at the picture on the sideboard and smiled at the family looking back at her. The mother and father seemed happy; although she couldn't see the mother very well because the face was smudged. The father had his arm around his partner, and they were looking adoringly at their two boys.

She'd found the picture when she'd first moved into the flat, and although she knew that she should have thrown it away, she'd kept it, because it reminded her of what could have been if she'd found the right man. Silly really.

As she walked along the pavement, Rebecca rubbed her tummy then burped, she'd eaten too much. Embarrassed, she apologised to herself and carried on walking, and as she did so, she admired the heavily decorated Christmas tree in the square.

After ten minutes, she stopped for a while and ordered herself a cup of mulled wine and a mince pie from the man in the van. As he handed her the cup she reached out to get it, but it fell to the floor and she looked at the vendor and said, ' I don't suppose I could get another one could I?' whereupon, he looked at her and shrugged, and she told him she didn't want the mince pie and left without paying.

'Hello Mr Davis,' she said happily as she watched her neighbour cross the road; but he looked at her and frowned, and then she watched him jump out of the way when a lorry nearly hit him.

Hello Mr Davis,' she said casually, and when he looked at her, she said, 'How are you Ben?' Then, without warning he slumped to the floor and she knelt to help him, and realising that he couldn't breathe, she went to administer the kiss of life, but was pushed out of the way when the paramedics arrived and took over from her.

She waited for a while, but sadly, he was pronounced dead at the scene. Rebecca knew that she should feel sorry for the old man, but she didn't feel anything for him, and she had no idea why? Feeling compelled to move on, she left the scene and continued walking towards the main square.

'Four bags of chestnuts and a cup of mulled wine please Bob.'
Bob smiled at her and she nodded and said, 'Just make it one bag.'
'Will do,' Bob said, and Rebecca was about to take the chestnuts off him when the man behind her pushed her out of the way. People were so rude nowadays.

Half an hour later and Rebecca decided to head back home. Mainly because she couldn't remember where she was going. It was gone 11pm now and she was starting to feel nervous when some of the streetlights went out. Nervously, she upped her pace and started walking towards the bus shelter that was still lit.

She stood there for a while, wondering what to do next. There weren't any busses at this time of night, and being Christmas day, there weren't any taxis either and she was getting worried. Then thankfully, she saw a group of ladies walking towards her and asked if she could accompany them, and one of them nodded and she followed on behind them.

Thankfully, she was able to walk with them to her apartment block and when she looked up at the window, she saw Mrs Smith standing there. Hastily, she took her mobile out of her handbag and rang the landlord who answered immediately.

'Mr Granger, it's Rebecca West. I know it's Christmas day, but I really need to talk to you about Mrs Smith, she's taking liberties and it's not fair. I know she's lonely, but her and that cat are starting to make a nuisance of themselves. Mr Granger, are you there?'

'Rebecca,' she heard somebody whisper and turned around.
'Do I know you? Only, you look familiar?'
'Yes Rebecca, you do. May I ask where you were going tonight?'
Puzzled, she said, 'I have no idea, I only know that I had to be somewhere, but I don't know where and suddenly, I felt compelled to come home.'
'Do you know my name?'
'I'm not sure, but I think it might be Simon.'
'That's right. Are you married?'
'Yes, No! I don't think so...'

Simon took her hand in his and led her upstairs to her flat, and when she saw Mrs Smith sitting on the sofa, she said angrily, 'Get out of here,' and she took a step back when the cat ran at her.

'She can't hear you,' Simon said kindly.

'I didn't know that. Perhaps if I had, I wouldn't have treated her so badly.'

Simon smiled, then said, 'Mrs Smith is your mother, this is her house. The boys were sleeping here the night we had the accident.

'I don't understand this, what's happening? I've never been married.'

Simon handed her the picture and she looked down at it. Simon was in the picture with the lady whose face was smudged and sitting down in front of them were the children, and they did look familiar, but she couldn't recall why.

'I don't know who you are, and I have no idea who those children are, what are you trying to do to me?'

Simon kissed her on the lips and the lonely part of her kissed him back, and suddenly, she remembered the smell of him, the taste of him and his touch.

He looked down at her, smiled and said, 'You remember, don't you?'

Crying softly to herself she said, 'It's starting to become clearer. Where are the children?'

'They're sleeping, your mum is taking care of them.'

'Have they opened their presents yet?'

'They did that this morning. It's been two years now, it's time to go. They are happy, you've done your job.'

'Can I see them?'

' Sure,' he said happily, and after putting the picture back on the hall table, he took her hand and walked with her to the bedroom and while her mother made hot chocolate in the kitchen, Simon guided Rebecca into the children's bedroom, held her close and they stayed that way for a while, until the children started to stir.'
'What happened?'

'It was Christmas day, and we were on our way back from your sisters, when we were involved in a car accident on the corner of the street where that man sells the hot chestnuts. Thankfully, the children were pulled free, but we weren't so lucky. I accepted that fact, but you couldn't until today. It's time to let go.'
'What if I don't want too?'
'Then you'll always be lonely, and you will repeat Christmas day again and again, and you'll be miserable, do you want that?'
'Of course not. How do I let go?'
'Just hold on to me and it will happen naturally. I'm sorry that you've been on your own for such a long time, come with me now.'

Rebecca looked at her children, Benny had a smile on his face and Stephen was cuddling his teddy, and they looked content.
She looked up at Simon and smiled, then held him tightly and slowly, they faded away.

'Can we have pancakes this morning nanny?' Benny and Stephen said in unison as they ran into the kitchen, and their nan smiled.
'Of course, pop and get dressed and they'll be ready in a few minutes.'

With that, they ran into their bedroom.

Mrs Smith walked into the hallway, picked up the leaflet off the floor, then stood up and looked at the picture frame on the table. Carefully, she moved it back to its original place and smiled.

Time for a Change

It was Christmas eve and Gertrude Alexandria Dooberry, was sitting in the park, watching her husband sail his model boat. She had been doing the same thing every Sunday and every other Monday for 20 years, ever since he'd retired at the ripe old age of 50. He'd been planning his early retirement for years, and after being left a sizable amount of money in a friend's will, he had retired with some money in the bank. Not that she was moaning, after all, he paid all the bills.

Sunday mornings, whatever the weather, she would pack some sandwiches and a flask of coffee and put it in the back of the van, whilst Dan Dooberry got his toy boat ready. Then they would drive for two hours until they were in the countryside, so that he could play with ten other pensioners who thought it was ok for grown men to play with toy boats.

When they were first married, she had mentioned that she would like to go out on the occasional Sunday, and he'd given her a menacing look and ever since then, she had just gone along with it. She'd accepted it as being a part of him. Besides, her charity knitting and looking after the children had kept her busy, until now. They'd all flown the nest and it was just her and him, and she couldn't imagine anything more frustrating.

Over the years, she'd come to accept his little foibles, but lately, at the grand old age of seventy, she didn't know how much more she could take. When he got up in the morning, he would take an hour to find something to wear. Then he would go downstairs and have two slices of brown toast with marmalade and a cup of tea, the same thing he'd been eating every morning for the last 40 years and it was getting on her nerves - watching him suck away at his toast like a tortoise.

Then, every day when they were at home, at exactly 11am he would go to his man shed and tinkle with his boat for three hours, leaving her to her own devises. However, she loved that time of the day because she could watch her favourite programmes on the telly.

At 2pm, he would saunter into the front room and watch a tv movie while she started the dinner and then, at 6pm precisely, having woofed down his dinner, he would walk upstairs to his study and spend the rest of the evening on the computer, and after she'd taken up his hot chocolate, he retired to his room. Oh yes! They had separate rooms, had done for over ten years.

Saturday, a week before Christmas and her daughters were coming over for Sunday dinner and she couldn't wait. She just hoped that their father would take some interest in them, at least for half an hour.
'What time are they coming over,' Dan asked, as he slumped down on to his recliner and pressed the remote.'
'They should be here in half an hour, be nice to them.'

'I'll try, but you know we don't get on.'
'And we know whose fault that is, don't we?'
'Don't start that again. We're both to blame. I should have spent more time with them, and you shouldn't have spoilt them rotten.'

Gertrude bit her lip and tutted, like she always did when he was getting on her nerves. The reason Dan and their daughters didn't get on, was because he'd wanted sons, and they'd never lived up to his expectations. Even though one of them was a doctor, and the other was a lawyer.

Which was a silly attitude to have, seeing that he had never been to university and had driven a taxi all his life; because he didn't have the courage to try something new. He was a small-minded man who was jealous of his own daughters.
'I'm not going to be here long, I'm meeting George down the pub, then we're off to look at a new boat.
'God forbid you care about someone other than yourself,' she mumbled.
'What did you say?'
'I said, they should be here any minute. Open a bottle of bubbly, will you?'
'You need to watch your tongue woman.'
'I don't ever stop holding my tongue,' she said bitterly, then went in search of the wine, because she knew he wouldn't do it.

'Hey mum,' Charlotte said, as she kissed her on the cheek and cuddled her.
Gertrude kissed her and said, 'Where's your sister?'
'I'm sorry mum, she says she can't bear to see him. Oh mum! Why don't you move in with me? There's only me

and Geoff and little Sam. We have room, the house is too big for us. Please mum.'
Lovingly she said, 'How many times must I tell you. I don't want to be a burden. You've got a great life, and you don't want me hanging around.'
'I do. I love you mum.'
Patting her daughter's hand, she said, 'I love you too, don't worry, I'm ok. Now Shush, here's your dad.'

'Charlotte,' her father said abruptly.
'How are you dad?'
'Good, I'm sorry I can't stay, I've got to meet a mate down the pub. It was good seeing you.' Then looking at Gertrude he said, 'Don't wait up.'
'Make yourself comfortable at the table love and I'll bring in the dinner.'

'Mum, why do you let him treat you like that?'
'Don't worry about me. I'm fine, plus, I have a plan.'
'What sort of plan?'
'You'll see.'
'That's ominous.'
'Eat your dinner.'
After dinner, they watched a movie together and cuddled up on the sofa, then just before the pub closed, Charlotte went home.

'Did you have a nice evening dear,' Gertrude asked, as she handed him his hot chocolate.
'Yes, I've bought another boat, I went halves with Geoff.'
'That's nice. I just remembered, I won't be able to come with you on Monday, I have to babysit.'
'Those kids put on you too much.'

'I love spending time with our grandchild, it's a shame you don't.'
'Don't start, I'll be on the computer for a bit, then I'm going to bed.'
'You've only just come in.'
'I can't stand your nagging.'
'Ok, off you go then.'
'Why are you disrespecting me?'
'How do you mean?'
'You're being sarcastic, you have been all day.'
Smirking, she said, 'Have I dear?'
'I'm not putting up with this, Goodnight.'
'Night dear.'

Gertrude laughed as she heard him stomp up the stairs. Perhaps, if she'd talked like that more often, her girls wouldn't be estranged from their father, and she wouldn't have been a doormat. However, she was going to make up for that. First, she had to ring her daughters, for they were part of the plan.

Just Desserts

Gertrude watched as Dan drove off then smiled, then she picked up her suitcase and walked towards the back gate to where the taxi was waiting.

Standing on the deck of the cruise ship, Gertrude watched her daughters and her grandchild walking towards her, and she smiled; she'd never been so happy.
'What's this all about mum?' Shelley asked.
'I'm treating everyone to a Christmas cruise, and when we get home, I'll show you my new flat. Don't worry about work, your husbands have sorted that out.'
Worried now, Charlotte said, 'How can you afford this?'

'Don't worry, I won a bit on the lottery.'
'What did dad say?'
'He doesn't know. It's time for me to move on.'
'I'd love to see his face when he realises your gone. Oh mum, we are so happy for you.'
Then they all cuddled.

As Gertrude watched her daughters playing in the pool, she smiled. If only she could have done this earlier. But then, the opportunity had never been there before. Dan was so tight when it came to money and hoarded it for himself. Until one day, while he was at the doctors, she went into his study and turned on his computer. He was so sure of himself, that he'd left all his passwords in a book by the side of the computer.

She'd looked through his history and had come across some bank accounts she didn't know he had. When she'd investigated further, she found that there were three. One contained fifty thousand, one contained one hundred thousand and the third, contained four hundred thousand pounds and that had made her so angry, that she plotted her revenge immediately.

She'd set up a bank account in her name, and via online banking, she had transferred all his money into her bank account. At one stage, she was going to leave him a small amount but decided against it. Throughout their marriage, she'd had to beg him for money for the simple things in life such as; shoes and clothes for the children; school trips and days out.

She still couldn't believe the audacity of the man. He'd said that he'd inherited twenty thousand pounds and had given her a thousand. At the time, she thought he was being generous and had thought that maybe he did have a heart, how wrong she'd been.

She just wished she could have been there when he'd discovered what she'd done, but obviously, she couldn't, for she valued her life. For the first time in her life, she was happy.

She no longer loathed boats because this cruise was going to be the making of her.
'Mum, dads on the phone,' Shelley said, as she opened the cabin door.
Gertrude shook her head.
'He's going mad, you better talk to him,' she said, not sure whether to cut him off.
'Dan, what is it?' Gertrude asked sweetly.
'Where are you?'
'I'm leaving you Dan.'
'Don't be stupid, where's my dinner... and you haven't done the dishes, or the hoovering, where are you?'
Gertrude smiled, it was obvious he hadn't been on his computer today and she sniggered to herself.

I've got to go, why don't you go and play on your computer, there's an email from somebody called Fleur, she's asking you if you want your usual. If so, it's going to cost you an extra £60.00 because she can't find the right oil. Also, there should be a message from the bank, you're overdrawn, or you will be.'

Gertrude laughed when the phone went dead and threw her daughters mobile phone out of the porthole.
'Sorry about that, I'll get you a new one.'

'Are you ready to go to dinner mum?'
'Give me a minute. I'll see you there.'
Shelley kissed her on the cheek and left, and Gertrude walked to the drawer and pulled out two envelopes.

Sitting at the dinner table with her family, Gertrude smiled and said, 'It's nearly Christmas day, but I'm going to give you your presents now, curtesy of your father.'
'Dad's bought us a present; Is he sick or something,' Charlotte said, and Shelley laughed.
Charlotte and Shelley took the envelopes off their mother and opened them and they both cried. She had given them one hundred thousand pounds each.
'Hopefully, that will make up for all the holidays, birthday and Christmas presents you didn't get, because your father was too tight.'
Raising her glass, Gertrude looked at them all and said, 'Let's raise a toast to your father.'
They all raised their glasses and Gertrude said, 'Merry Christmas Dan.'

A Christmas to Remember

'You have to go to Beth's Christmas party,' Stephanie said, giving her a look that meant she was serious.
'I can't be bothered.'
'You need to get out more, you're turning into a right slob. When was the last time you showered?'
'Just go will you and let me wallow for a bit.'
'He's been gone for three months; you've got to get back to work and get on with your life. I bet he's not skulking around thinking about you.'

'I don't care. He was my first love and you can't expect me to get over him just like that.'
'I didn't want to tell you this, but he's moved in with his bit of stuff.'
'I already know. June from the accounts department told me.'
'The cow, she's always hated you.'
'You're not leaving until I agree to go, are you?'
'No.'
'Alright. I'll go, but only if you go with me.'
'Of course, anyway, I have to pick you up in case you change your mind.'

After Stephanie had gone, Andrea walked into the bathroom to have a shower. Her friend was right, it was time to move on.
Andrea rushed out of the shower and answered the phone; it was him.
'Can I come over,' Chris whispered, and she sighed.
'Why?'
'I miss us.'
Against her will, she started to cry and slammed the phone down.

Of course, she wanted to see him, but what would it achieve? He had cheated on her and left her skint; after living together for six years. If he'd done it once, he could do it again and she didn't want to be hurt like that again. She'd been on sickness benefit and had lost her job because of him. No! She had to get her life back somehow and move on.

Andrea opened the letter, hoping she'd got the job, but sadly it was another rejection and she put it with the other ten on the shelf, then picked up her mobile when it rang.
'Can I come over. I really need to see you. I've made a terrible mistake. I love you. Please let me come over.'
'What's the matter Chris, have you left her too?'
There was a long pause and then he said begrudgingly, 'She left me and I'm living at my brother's house.'
'What do you want to see me about? I'm not having you back, if that's what you're hoping.'
'We were together for six years, you can't let that go down the pan, we were good together, you can't deny that.'
'We had some fantastic times, that's why it was a shock when you left me.'
'It was the biggest mistake of my life. I was flattered that somebody that young fancied me.'
Andrea felt sick and said angrily, 'We're the same age for god sake.'
'I'm so sorry Andrea, please give me another chance.'
'I'm sorry Chris, I never want to feel like this again. Don't ring me again.'

This time Chris put the phone down. She didn't cry, after all, this wasn't the first time he'd had an affair, it was just the first time he'd got caught.
She'd spent a lot of time on Chris and she couldn't afford to waste any more of her life.

The Interview

'Good day Miss Green, please take a seat.'
'Thank you, please call me Andrea.'

'So, Andrea, you have a great reference from your previous employer. He really regrets you going. Why did you leave?'
'I'm not one for beating around the bush. My partner of six years left me, and I was devastated and fell apart for a while. If you are worried it will happen again, don't be, because I've learnt my lesson.'
'Oh dear, so, you're off men for good then, that's a shame,' he said, and for a minute, she felt as if he was flirting with her and it made her feel good, and she smiled and was pleased when he smiled back. He was attractive and it was disconcerting.

'Well, I'm sorry to hear that, you're not the first person to lose someone they love. I'm sorry, I digress.'
'I am computer literate; I get on well with people and I feel that I will be perfect for the role of receptionist in your firm. I also have six years' experience of working with the public and a good reference from my previous employer.'

Looking down at his notes, then scrutinising her a little he said, 'I have a few more people to see, but I'll let you know either way this evening around six. You do have an answer phone?'
Patience not being one of her strongpoints, she nodded then said, 'Can you give me any idea of my chances?'
He laughed then said, 'That wouldn't be fair on the other applicants, but I can tell you this. You certainly left an impression on me.'
Downhearted, she stood up when he did and shook his hand.
'Thank you for seeing me,' she said, then she walked out the door and into the street.

'Well?' Stephanie asked, as she sat opposite Andrea in the coffee shop.
Taking her coffee off the tray she looked at her and said, 'I've no idea because I ranted on and on like I normally do.'
'You're too honest for your own good that's your trouble.'
'I've given up looking for work until after Christmas. If Chris hadn't cleared out our savings account, I would have loved to have gone away for Christmas.'
'I could always lend you the money.'
'No, it's ok. I'll be fine. I'll get my decorations up and stock up on loads of goodies and curl up on the settee and watch all the Christmas movies on the telly.'
'You can always come to ours for Christmas, it may be a bit noisy, what with my six brothers coming home for Christmas, but it will be fun.'
'Don't worry about me, I'll be fine.'
Stephanie leant forward, kissed her on the cheek and said, 'I'm always here if you need me.'

Andrea picked up her mobile and put it on the coffee table, picked up her coffee, and waited patiently for the phone to ring. It was five to six and she was praying that he would ring her as soon as possible to put her out of her misery, but once six fifteen came, she put the phone back in her bag and walked into the bedroom and lay on the bed. She wasn't tired, just fed up.

In the morning, she checked her home phone and her mobile but there was nothing and reluctantly, she walked into the kitchen to prepare her breakfast. She'd decided to have a full English today. Being Saturday, she and Stephanie were going clothes shopping and she needed as much energy as she could get.

You've got to buy it, it really suits you,' Stephanie said, then added, 'I'm going to buy it for you, it will be your Christmas present. You can wear it to Beth's Christmas party.'

Andrea put the dress back on the rack and cuddled her friend and said, 'I'm okay, I appreciate the offer, but I've got a few black dresses that I've only worn once, they will do.'

'You're so stubborn.'

'I'm responsible that's all. You better get going, Steve will be picking you up soon.'

Looking at her watch she said, 'Darn, he finished work an hour ago, I'd better run. Don't forget its Beth's party next Saturday, me and Steve will pick you up at eight. I'll be angry if you don't come. Promise me you'll come.'

'I promise, it will give me something to look forward too.'

Andrea watched her leave the coffee shop and decided to have another drink and a toastie. She didn't want to go home, after all, she had nothing to go home for.

The toastie went down well and she was drinking the hot chocolate when she noticed Mr Ben Rogers walk into the coffee shop and head for the counter.

He was dressed casually in jeans and a Christmas Jumper and she had to admit to herself that she fancied him.

'Hey,' he said happily as he walked over to her table.

Andrea smiled and put down her cup, looked up and said, 'Hello Mr Rogers.'

'This is the only available seat, mind if I sit here,' he asked, sitting opposite her as he said it, and she nodded her head.

'I'm Ben. Welcome to our company.'

'I'm sorry, what did you say?'

'Welcome to the firm.'

'I got the job?'
'Why do you say it like that?'
'You said you would ring either way and you didn't.'
'My receptionist should have got in touch with you. You will be receiving the official offer soon and will be starting on the 7th.'

'That's great. Thank you.'
'No problem, you were the best candidate. How are you?'
'I'm good, especially now I've got a job, why do you ask?'
'Do you fancy going to a party next Saturday?'
She was smiling so hard that she couldn't say anything, then she remembered she was going out with Stephanie. Disappointed, she said, 'I'm sorry, I promised to go out with my friend.'
'Perhaps another night.'
'Thank you. I'd like that. What about tonight?'
He smiled, took a sip of his coffee and said, 'Sorry, I'm busy, which reminds me, I've got to get back to work. It was nice seeing you,' and with that, he got up and left without saying goodbye.

The Party

After putting on several outfits she'd finally decided on a short black dress and some two-inch sparkly shoes, and she was pleased with how she looked. She'd decided to keep her long brown hair down because it was in good condition and she wanted to show it off; it was her best asset.

Thankfully, Stephanie and her boyfriend arrived on time to pick her up and they got to the party at around half eight and it was in full flow, and even though Stephanie's sister Beth was busy, she had come out to greet them.

Now, Stephanie and her boyfriend were dancing to a slow dance, and she was sat in the conservatory and was on her third Bacardi and coke and was starting to relax.
'Hello Andrea, it's nice to see you.'
Andrea looked up to see Ben looking down at her and unable to control her feelings she smiled, then said, 'Fancy a dance?'
'I'd love too, but I'm not sure my friend would like it.' Then he pointed to a woman in the corner and she knew, there was no way she would ever be able to compete with someone as beautiful as her.

Andrea watched him walk away and chastised herself for being a walk over. He was the first person she'd found attractive since splitting up with Chris and she was ready to throw herself at him. She hadn't realised how lonely she was, and a tear came to her eye.

'Good news, my friend had to leave. I mean, I didn't want her to miss the party, but her husband is in the army and he's just surprised her by coming home early,' Ben said.
Hastily wiping her tears away, Andrea said, 'Are you in a relationship?'
'No, are you?'
She smiled as he sat down by her side and said, 'No, I got dumped.'
'Do you want to get out of here. I've got a bottle of champagne back at the flat and some left-over snacks.'
'I should say no, but as it's Christmas Eve, I'm going to say yes.'

'You can sleep in the spare room if you want to stay over. I'll take you home tomorrow. I'd love some company tonight.'
'Me too, I'll get my coat.'

Ben opened the champagne and brought out the snacks and laid them on the floor by the log fire. Then he got some bean bags from the bedroom and scattered them around, and they sat down. Then he reached for the tree lights and turned them on and for the first time in ages she felt safe and warm, and wished the night would never end. It was as if her dreams were coming true.

She took a sip of the champagne and turned to him and said, 'You've done this before haven't you?'
'Not as often as you think.'
'Have you ever been married?'
'Can't we just enjoy tonight. Do we really need to do this?'
'No, but I was hoping to get to know you a bit better.'

'Putting his glass on the table, he turned to her and said, 'Look, I'm sorry if I've misled you. I'm not after anything serious, I was just hoping for company.'
'She kissed him gently on the cheek and said wistfully, I understand. Do you want to put a DVD on?'
He instantly did as she asked and put a rom com in the player and sat back with her, whereupon, she cuddled into him and he held her to him. She could smell the expensive aftershave he had on and smiled. He smelt good.

As they sat there, drinking the champagne and enjoying the film, Ben started to stroke her hair and she was loving it, then before she knew it, they were making love in front of the fire and she'd never felt so loved, even with Chris, who's idea of sex was a two minute rub and then the act itself. Ben was a thoughtful lover and they couldn't get enough of each other. He was the best Christmas present she'd ever had and when he led her into his bedroom she went willingly.

The following morning, she woke up to find him sitting up in bed looking down at her.
'You are beautiful.'
She smiled and he kissed her on the lips, and she pulled him down on top of her.
Pushing himself up, he said, 'Sorry, I've an errand to run. I'll be back in a couple of hours. Will you stay for dinner?'
'Sure, would you like company?'
'No, I've got to deliver some presents to my mum's house for my nieces and nephews. She only lives down the road, but she will make me stay for a while. Which I don't mind because I haven't seen her in ages. Make yourself comfortable, the coffees on and there is some bread in the cupboard.'
'You better go, the sooner you go, the sooner you will be back, and we can carry on from where we left off,' she said, smirking a little, and pleased that he'd invited her to dinner.

Four hours later and he still wasn't back, and she wondered if she should go home. Perhaps this was his way of saying the date was over. She decided to give him another hour then head home. Sadly, another two hours later and he still wasn't back, and it was then that she realised it was probably a one-night stand - it was time to go.

When she got home, she put on her heating and sat in the bed until her flat had warmed up, and while she waited, she thought about Ben. She liked him. He was honest, kind and considerate and had told her right from the start that he didn't want anything serious and she was pleased that he'd told her that, because it meant she didn't have to feel guilty; even though she would have liked to see him again. He was the best Christmas present she'd ever had, because he'd made her feel good about herself and knowing that another man found her attractive, gave her the strength to move on.

The day after boxing day, she opened the door to find Chris sitting in the hallway.
'Chris! What are you doing here?'
'I miss us Andrea, I should never have left you. Can we talk?'
'I'm sorry, you've strayed away from home too often. I can't take you back, the trust has gone, and I don't love you anymore.'
'Of course, you do. We're soul mates. Have you got someone else?'
'I did meet someone but that's over now. It showed me that I am worthy of a man's love and not just someone to come home to when they've finished with their bit of stuff.'
'I love you.'

'You may love me, but you're not in love with me. I deserve someone better. You're only feeling down because you've been jilted, you'll get over it. I thought I'd never get over you, but I have. I've got the rest of my life ahead of me and I'm determined to live it. I should thank

you for leaving me really, otherwise I would never have known what was out there.'
'You're a right bitch, what the hells happened to you. You've changed.'
'I've finally got a voice. I suppose I should thank you for that. Now if you'll excuse me, I'm going out.'
Reluctantly, Chris walked towards the stairs, while Andrea took the lift.

Andrea was just about to step into the shower when the doorbell went and she wrapped her towel around her and walked to the front door, it was Ben.
'Hey,' he said sheepishly, and she smiled.
'How are you?'
'Good, thank you. Do you fancy coming out for lunch today?'
'Not really, I'm just about to get into the shower, then I've got things to do.'
'Perhaps another time?'
'I'd like that. Now, if you'll excuse me, I really need to take a shower. I've been running and I'm not at my best.'
'Ok, any idea when you'll be free?'
'I'm free any time after today.'
'What about tomorrow morning, I'll treat you to breakfast.'
'Thank you, I'd like that,' she said, not wanting to sound too excited, for inside, she had butterflies in her stomach. 'I'll see you tomorrow then,' she said, as she closed the door behind her.

Having finished her shower, she walked into the kitchen to make herself a sandwich and grumbled to herself. She wished she'd let Ben in. She was trying not to sound too eager and now she was going to be bored out of her head all day.

Then the doorbell went, and she slammed her plate on the table and walked to the door. This time, she wouldn't let her ex off lightly, she was going to tell him a few home truths.
'I've told you it's over…'
Ben laughed, and she looked at him and said, 'Sorry, I didn't mean you.'
'I should hope not. The thing is, I'm missing you already and I'm hungry, any chance of a bite to eat?'
'Only if you like stale bread with a bit of cheese slapped in the middle.'
Smirking, he said, 'That's just the way I like it.'

Ben followed her into the kitchen and sat at the table, and watched her put together a sandwich, and when she handed it to him, he said, ' That's not enough, I'm going to need a lot more than that, if I am going to last the night.' Getting the gist of what he was saying, she took his hand and led him into the bedroom.
She liked him, so why not? After all, this was the season of good will to all men.

The New Job

The 7th January and it was Andrea's first day in her new job, and she was enjoying it. Although it was January the place was busy, and she was pleased. The busier the better as far as she was concerned. The part time receptionist was fun to be around, and she felt as if she'd been there for years.

'Will you come to the office to sign your contract please,' Ben said, and Andrea walked around the desk and followed on behind him, while Hazel held the fort.

Once inside the office, Ben pulled Andrea towards him and said, 'Are you coming to my place tonight?'
'You know it's my flat tonight. We've got to talk.'
He laughed and said light-heartedly, 'Are you dumping me?'
'I will if you don't keep your promise.'
Smirking he said, 'I was missing you, after all, I haven't seen you since breakfast.'
'You promised to leave me alone when I'm at work. If you don't keep to that promise, I'll have to find a new job.'
Disheartened he said, 'Alright, when can I talk to you at work?'
'You can say hello and goodbye and talk to me like you would any other employee. I don't want people to know I'm sleeping with the boss.'
'Alright, I'm sorry. You better get back now just in case somebody suspects.'
She laughed, pushed him against the desk and passionately kissed him, then five minutes later she said, 'We've got steak tonight, is that ok.'
'Sure.' With that, she took the lift down to the foyer and when the doors opened, Ben walked into the elevator and she smiled, as he took her in his arms and kissed her.

How the hell was she going to be able to hide their relationship with him being so demonstrative all the time. Then she smiled again. Ever since she'd met him, she'd been smiling.

'Are you and the boss an item?' Hazel asked, and Andrea smiled.
'Are we?' Ben said, as he walked over to them, leant on the counter and looked at her seriously.
Andrea frowned and said, 'I suppose so.'
'Good,' the receptionist said excitedly. Then she went around to the other side of the counter and hugged Ben and said, 'Ben's my brother, welcome to the family.'
Smirking, Ben said, 'Still want to keep it a secret?'
'Funny, now if you don't mind, I need to get on with my job. See you later.'

Head down, Ben walked away, pretending to be hurt, and as he was just about to get into the lift, he turned to look at her and whispered, 'I love you.'
She mimed back that she loved him too, and was half tempted to run after him, but she had to remain professional, no matter how much she was distracted by him.

After all, it was early days, and she didn't want to put her job in jeopardy, if what they had now was only a Christmas crush.

Snow and Clause

'Name?' the receptionist asked, without looking up.
'Miss Snow,' she replied, as she waited for that oh so predictable reaction.
Looking at her now with a huge smirk on his face, the receptionist said, 'May I have your first name please?'
'Winter.'

'Winter Snow,' he said, in a squeaky voice, trying his hardest not to laugh.
'OK, you've had your fun, now get my keys please.'
'You have to admit it's funny,' he said, as he turned around, took her keys off the hook and handed them to her.
'I can see the funny side yes, but after twenty- five years it gets a bit boring.'
'Shall I fetch someone to carry your bags up?'
'No thanks, but if you could send a snowball and some Turkey sandwiches up to my room, I'd be grateful.'
The man laughed so hard that his sides hurt, and he had to sit down, and not feeling the joy of the season, Winter turned her back on him and walked to the lift.

'Can I help you sir,' the receptionist asked, as the man walked up to the counter.
With some trepidation he said, 'Mr Clause.'
'Really, the man said, as he put his hand over his mouth to hide the smirk on his face.
'Nick Clause.'
The receptionist could no longer control himself and almost fell of his seat when he started to laugh hysterically.
'What on earth are you doing Ken?'
Seeing his boss staring down at him brought him to his senses and he got up and handed Nick the keys and said, 'Do you need help with your bags sir?'
'No, I'm fine, thank you. But I'd like room service if that's OK?'
'Let me guess, a snowball and a Turkey sandwich?'
'Funny! I'll have a cider and some cheese sandwiches please.'

'What are you doing Ken, a word please,' his boss said, as he watched the man walk to the lift.
'What on earth is wrong with you?'
'I think I'm being set up. Winter Snow and a Nick Clause have just signed in.'

Winter looked out of her bedroom window at the view and smiled. She loved Weymouth and she loved the beach. It didn't matter that it was the middle of December and raining, for she'd brought plenty of waterproofs.

Nick opened the window and smiled when he felt the rain brush against his skin and the wind caress his face. He loved winter and what came with it. He loved the cold, hot chocolate, mulled wine, Turkey, the lot.
Or rather he had. Since mum and dad had died, and his fiancé had left him, Christmas just didn't seem the same. Still, he was going to have a week off from all the festivities to wind down.

As Nick passed through the foyer, he couldn't help but spot the good- looking young woman sitting on the sofa. She wasn't his normal type, he usually didn't go for women with long brown hair and blue eyes, but for some reason, he was drawn to her and when she looked up, it was as though he felt compelled to go over and would have, if someone hadn't called his name. He turned around and came face to face with the receptionist.
'A Mr Barratt called, could you ring him back.'
He sighed; his deputy should know better than to ring him while he was on holiday.

As Winter walked along the esplanade, she thought about the young man standing by the reception desk, somehow, she felt drawn to him, but had no idea why. Since she'd finished with Philip, six months ago, she'd made a pact with herself, never to enter into another relationship for at least two years.

She'd picked two years, because she would grieve over that dead-beat ex-boyfriend for about a year, then use the second year to prove to herself that she didn't need a man.

The Meeting

'There's been a mix up with the bookings,' the manager said, as Nick answered the door to him.
'And...'
'Would you mind sharing your table with another guest, we haven't enough room in the dining room. I've asked around, but nobody's too keen on moving.'
'I've come away for a mini break to get away from people. Can't you find anyone else?'
'There will be a 30% discount off your bill and seeing that you're in one of our best suites, that will be a hefty amount.'
'I'll give it a go for tonight, but then you'll have to find a table for them tomorrow because I've come away for a bit of peace and quiet.'
'Thank you, Mr Clause.'
'Just tonight mind.'
The manager nodded and Nick sighed and went for his shower.

'I'm sorry Miss Snow, but we're a bit lacking in space, it's just until we get the bookings sorted. The manager will give you 40% off your bill. We had a late booking from a young family, and they could only come this week.

Apparently, they've been saving up all year for this and I didn't have the heart to turn them away.'
'That's it, pull at my heart strings why don't you. Alright, just for tonight.'
'Thank you miss,' Ken said, smiling from ear to ear as he walked to the lift.

Nick walked into the restaurant and the manager walked over to him and showed him to his table. The other guest hadn't arrived. If he timed it right, he could order his food straight away and be gone before they got there. Thankfully, it was a table by the window which cheered him up, because there was a beautiful view across the bay.

Winter didn't want to walk into the restaurant alone, and as she approached the door, she turned around to see if there were any food servers around. In the end, she walked up to the reception desk.

Ken looked up from the guest book and smiled, then walked into the restaurant with her and over to where Nick was sitting. When Nick saw her, he stood up.
Ken pulled her chair out and she sat down, and Nick did too.
'I'm Nick,' he said, putting out his hand and she took it and said, 'Winter.'
'That's a great name, where do you come from?'
'It's a little place in Cumbria called Ivy Tree. You?'
'Christmas Cross in Shropshire.'
'That's a pretty name. Well, it looks like we're stuck with each other.'
Nick didn't say anything and smiled; he couldn't wait to get to know her.

As Winter watched him eat, she was pleased to find that he wasn't a messy eater and unlike her ex, who ladled his food into that big fat mouth of his, Nick was a tidy eater. He'd already ticked one box. Not that she had boxes.

Neither said anything while they ate, not because they didn't want to, but because they didn't want to embarrass themselves if they still had their greens between their teeth. Towards the end of the meal, they each went to the toilet to check, and when they were drinking their coffees, they both felt relaxed enough to speak.

'What do you do for a living Nick?'
'Don't laugh, I own a toy store.'
'I'm a weather girl.'
'Wow! That's so cool.'
'It's out of the ordinary I grant you, but it has its downside. The early mornings can be a killer sometimes.'
'I can imagine, are you on national telly?'
'Regional, I just sort of fell into the job. My friend worked there, and they were short one day and asked me to step in.'
'That was lucky.'
'I guess so. I wouldn't have put you down as a sales assistant.'
'It was my father's store, I'm in the process of bringing it into the twenty first century.'

A short silence followed while they ate their dessert and when they were on their second cup of coffee, Nick said, 'What are you doing here?'
'I just needed to get away for a while, Christmas is a big family occasion at our house, and I need a rest before it begins.'

'Me too. I'm rushed off my feet over the Christmas period. Fancy a walk on the esplanade?'
'I'd like that, thank you. I'll just get my coat.'

As they walked along the esplanade, the biting wind forced them to go back and dishevelled and shivering, they took their coats off and sat by the roaring fire in the lounge, next to a huge Christmas tree.

'That's a shame, I've never been to Weymouth before, I was hoping to see something off it.'
Winter smiled, looked at him and said cheerfully, 'If we get some brollies we can go exploring tomorrow, I come here most years.'
'I'd like that, fancy a drink?'
With that, he went to the bar and came back with two huge hot chocolates.
She laughed when he handed it to her and said, 'I was expecting something stronger.'
'Perhaps we can have a night cap later.'
'I'd like that. So, what are you running away from?'
'That's a bit personal, can't we sit here and enjoy this place. After all, we'll be leaving in a few days, can't we just have fun.'
'Sure, sorry. My friends say I'm always intense, which is probably why my boyfriend left me.'
'I can't imagine anyone leaving you, you're charming.'
Winter blushed and whispered, 'If you think that's going to get me in your bed, you'd be right.'

Nick stood up and looking down at her said, 'What's going on here. We've only just met and you're talking about sleeping with me. I certainly don't need this. I don't want a

Christmas romance or a quickie, what the hell...' and with that, he strode out of the lounge.

Winter wiped the tears out of her eyes, picked up the cushion and cuddled it. She wasn't normally that forward. She supposed that she was lonely and suddenly, she'd never felt so embarrassed. She hadn't meant to say that, she wouldn't have normally, the words just seemed to slip out of her mouth. She would stick to her room for the rest of her stay or go home a few days early.

The following morning, Nick was sat in the dining room eating his breakfast thinking about the night before. He was deeply ashamed of his behaviour and when Winter came down for breakfast he intended to apologise. She had only said what he was thinking, and there was nothing wrong with that. In fact, after he'd left the room, he'd wanted to go back to her but had not given into his feelings, mores the pity, for he really liked her.

Looking out of her bedroom window, Winter watched as the rain drizzled down the pane of glass and sighed. She felt sick and embarrassed. It wasn't as if she'd had some wine and had loose lips. She'd meant what she'd said. She liked him. Which was strange, since the last thing she wanted was another relationship.

Winter opened the door to the concierge, and he handed her a bunch of flowers and said, 'Mr Clause asks if you would like to have breakfast with him this morning?'
'Tell him I'll be there in ten minutes, thank you.'

Ten minutes later and Winter was standing by the door of the lounge wondering whether to go in or not, because she felt embarrassed, but the decision was taken out of her hands when Nick walked over to her, took her hand in his and led her to their table.

She sat down and poured herself some tea and took a bite out of her toast, staring out of the window as she ate, waiting for him to start talking.
'I was so rude last night; will you forgive me?'
Looking at him now, she said politely,' I'm sorry too, I didn't mean to be so forward. I've been thinking about it all night. I'm not usually like that, I'm usually shy. I think it was the log fire and the tree, it was all so perfect that I got carried away.'
'The thing is, I was thinking the same thing as you, and it came as a bit of a shock when you said it first.'
Blushing and looking down at the table she whispered, 'I was just lonely I guess.'
He took her hand in his and said coyly, 'So you don't fancy me?'
She laughed then squeezed his hand and said, 'How could I possibly fancy someone as arrogant as you?'
'That's what I thought, fancy showing me the sights after breakfast, I've got a whole week.'
'I'd love to, but first, I need something inside me to keep me going.'
They looked at each other and he smirked, and she smiled and tutted.

As she got dressed, Winter thought about her unfaithful ex and smirked. To think, if he hadn't dumped her in that way, she wouldn't have come to this hotel to lick her wounds, and she wouldn't have found Nick. It was then that she decided she would send him a Christmas card, thanking him for dumping her. This was the closure she had been looking for. Suddenly, she was looking forward to the week ahead, whatever came of it, and she felt excited at the prospect of seeing Nick.

Nick put his shoes on then picked up the picture of his fiancée. To think, if she hadn't dumped him and he'd come here to get over her, he would never have met Winter. It was as if it was meant to be. Then he picked up his keys and wallet and headed out.

As Nick walked into the foyer, Winter's heart seemed to miss a beat, and when he took her hand in his, she felt as if she was floating on air. Was this what real love felt like?
'Are you alright?' Nick asked, and she looked up at him and nodded her head.
'I feel great, you?'
He pulled her towards him and kissed her gently on the lips and she responded eagerly, then she took a step back and he said, 'I've never felt this good. I feel heavy headed, my pulse is racing and I've no idea why.'
'Perhaps you like me?'
'Well, we've got a week to find out, or longer if we need it?'
Winter liked the 'longer' part of the sentence and smiled. Was this really happening?

Winter opened her eyes and looked around the room. She was in her bedroom in the hotel. She looked at the clock on the wall, it was ten to nine. Then she reached over to his side of the bed, but he wasn't there.

A solitary tear fell down her cheek when she realised, she'd been dreaming and frowning, she heaved herself of the bed and walked into the bathroom and had a shower, and as the water splashed over her body, she suddenly felt lonely. She was also afraid and unhappy, and that dream had given her hope for the first time in ages. Now, she was going to spend the week alone, as she suspected she would.

Putting on her bathrobe she walked back into the bedroom to find Nick lying naked on the bed with nothing but a piece of mistletoe to hide his modesty and she giggled.
'Where were you?'
'I popped out to get some snacks, I don't think we'll be leaving this bedroom this week, do you?'
Smiling, she let her robe fall to the floor and smiled when he looked at her adoringly.
'Merry Christmas,' he said, as he handed her the tickets and Winter looked down at them. He was taking her to the North Pole for two weeks in the new year.'
'You are kidding.'
'No, we are going to the North Pole in Oklahoma.'
She laughed and looked at him, and realising he was smirking she said, 'Funny.'

It was then that she realised, that this wasn't just a Christmas fling and she smiled, which wasn't lost on Nick who said, 'I hope you can get the time off work.'
'I've got a lot of leave owing to me, so that will be fine.'

As they slipped out of their clothes she said, 'Next, you're going to tell me that your toy shop is called Santa's Grotto.'
Taking her in his arms he said, 'That's another story,' and before she could say anything, he was kissing her and pulling her down onto the bed.

Santa Baby

Cheryl flicked through the channels but was disappointed to find that there were no Christmas films on. She'd taken a week off to get into the spirit of things and it was starting to be a bit of a let-down. She'd hung the decorations up, decorated the tree, made a Christmas cake and two batches of mince pies, and she was wondering what to do next when Bob, her ex rang her.
'Can I come over?'
'Why?'
'I've missed you.'
'Don't be absurd, I haven't heard from you in ages.'
'I still love you.'
'Your floozy has kicked you out, that's it isn't it. Well, don't think about coming here, because I'm not taking you back. I've already wasted six years of my life on you.'
'Just let me talk to you.'
The doorbell rang, which was her excuse to hang up and she said, 'I've got to go, someone's at the door.'

When she opened the flat door, she laughed. A man dressed up in a Santa suit was staring at her.
'Hi, I'm a Santa gram and I'm sorry to disturb you, but I'm lost.'
'Who are you looking for?'
'Melanie Brown.'
She lives at number six, it's on the next floor up.'
'Cheers, Merry Christmas.'
'Merry Christmas,' she said as she closed the door.

She took the mince pies off the tray and put them in some sealed containers; she would take them around to her mum's house tomorrow. Then she cheered up when she remembered that she and her mother were going Christmas shopping tomorrow and the following day, she and her sister were taking her twins to see Father Christmas, and later that same day, she and her bestie were having a girly night in. She'd forgotten all that and suddenly, her mood changed for the better.

'Darn,' she said, as she heard the doorbell go. She wiped her hands and walked to the front door. It was Santa again.
'How can I help?'
'I went to number six but there was nobody in.'
'She's probably changed the number on the door, she thinks that's funny and does that a lot. When you get out of the lift, whatever the number says, it's the first door on the left.'
'I thought I heard people giggling, but I thought they were up to no good, if you know what I mean,' then he smiled, and she laughed and closed the door.

Cheryl was trying to finish the washing up when the phone rang again and was disappointed to find that it was Bob.
'Please let me come over. I need to talk to you.'
'I don't want you here Bob. It took me a while to get over you, and I don't want to drag up memories.'
'I'm outside.'

Cheryl turned her mobile off and put it in her bag and answered the door, and sure enough, when she opened it, Bob was standing in front of her with a big bunch of

flowers in his hand, which she took from him and put on the side.
'Sit down, would you like a coffee,' she asked politely.
'No thanks, can we talk?'
Sitting comfortably on the sofa she turned to him and he said, 'We had some good times, didn't we?'
'Did we, when?'
'When we went on holiday to the South of France.'
'Oh yes, you had a good time with everything in a skirt while I was back at the hotel, if I remember correctly.'
'Maybe that wasn't a good example. What about that time we went to Disney World with your sister and the twins?'
'Yes, once again, you had a great time, running after every woman in the hotel. I think you managed to hook a few if I remember rightly. You've had chance after chance. We're finished.'

'I may be your only hope. After all, you're getting on a bit now aren't you?'
'Thanks for that. Now you've said your piece it's time for you to go.'
'I love you,' he said unhappily as he stood up and followed her to the door.
'I loved you once. I think that lasted for the first two weeks of our relationship, so thanks for that.'
'Since when have you got so hard.'
'I'm assertive, not hard. Finally, I'm able to say what I feel. Actually, I've got you to thank for that.'
'Cow.'
'You just couldn't keep the pretence up could you. Now that's the real you,' she said, as she opened the door and came face to face with Santa.

This was an opportunity she couldn't pass up and hoping he would go along with it she said, 'Hey.'
Then she took off Santa's beard, stood on tip toes and kissed Santa hard on the lips and he responded willingly and when it was over, she winked at him, turned to Bob and said, 'I think you need to go Bob, and as for me never finding anyone else, you're wrong there too.'

'You heard the lady,' Santa said, and with his tail between his legs, Bob left and as he walked down the corridor, he looked back to see Cheryl and Santa kissing and he felt sick. Despite his wayward ways, he'd never stopped loving her. Now, he had to go back to the floozy.

Once Bob was out of sight, she looked up at Santa and said, 'I'm sorry about that, that was my ex and I wanted to show him that I was still capable of getting a man. He wasn't exactly kind to me tonight.
'There must be plenty of men after you, look at you, you're drop dead gorgeous.'
She blushed and looked at the man behind the beard and smiled. He must have been around the same age as her and he was good looking; and she loved the smiley lines around his eyes.

'Well, thanks for playing a long, how did the gig go?'
'Very well, that's my last one, getting a little long in the tooth to still be doing this.'
'Why would you say that? You have a great body and are good looking.'
This time it was his turn to blush, and he said, 'That's the nicest thing anyone's said to me in a long time.'
'Thanks again, I'd better go in now it's getting late.'
'Sure, it was nice meeting you.'

Cheryl looked out of the window and watched Santa walk away and sighed. He seemed to have a great personality but just like all the good men in this world he was probably taken.

Half an hour later, she grumbled when she heard the doorbell go again, but this time, she was ready for Bob. However, it was Santa, or rather, the man who was pretending to be Santa. He'd taken off his disguise and was standing in front of her in stonewashed jeans and a Rudolph top and she smiled; he was even more handsome.

'This maybe a bit forward, but I was wondering, would you like to come to dinner at my house on Christmas Eve?' Sensing that he was serious, she said, 'I'd love to, thank you.'
He smiled and scribbled his address on a piece of paper with his phone number and gave it to her. He didn't live far from her, which was a bonus.
'Well, I'm meeting my brother for a Christmas drink, I'll see you around eight?'
'That's great,' she said shyly, and then she kissed him on the cheek and said, 'Thank you.'
'No, thank you. I'll see you soon.'

Cheryl looked out of the window and when he looked up at her and waved, she waved back and whispered to herself, Ho, Ho, Ho.

A less than Perfect Gift

Sandra and Robin watched with excitement as their grandfather gave out the presents, and after the last one was handed out, Sandra and Robin lay back in their chairs and took the lemonade and cake offered to them by their mother. She smiled at them and although they felt left out, because they hadn't been given a present, their mother's smile always cheered them up. Once again, by not giving them a present, even though her grandparents knew that they were coming, it reinforced the fact that her family looked upon them as outsiders.

Robin was too young to understand but Sandra wasn't, and when she looked out of the window towards the garden, she watched as her father put his arms around her mother when she started to sob. Mum and dad had to get married at a young age because her mother had fallen pregnant with her, and it had been frowned upon by everyone.

Then, when they moved over a hundred miles away from the family, they were ostracised and never felt part of the family. In later years, as she was growing up, Sandra became the butt of their jokes. They often remarked about her weight and the fact that she wore glasses and had part of a tooth missing. One aunt even remarked to the other that when she grew up, she would be fat, blind, and toothless. Which thankfully she wasn't.

Her mother was privy to those comments too. Sandra couldn't remember any of her family praising her mother. Meanwhile, they moaned about her marrying young and being pregnant at a young age, but ironically, her mother's marriage was the only one that had lasted.

That was over forty years ago, but Sandra would never forget how her family were treated on that day, and the way her mother's family had ostracised her mother. They thought she was weak, yet she was the strongest person Sandra knew. But of course, the family would have known that, if they had bothered to take the time to get to know her.

As for sisterly love, her sisters would often talk about her mother behind her back, and knowing that her mother knew that, had upset Sandra, and she was never able to bond with any of her mother's relations.

A Lesson learnt

'Is it ok if Andrew and Tammy come over, their mother and father are working, and I thought it would be good for them to come here.'
'Sure,' Sandra's husband said happily. Then he smiled, he had no say in the matter really. When it came to Christmas, Sandra had her own set of rules and everybody had to obey them. That was the only time of year she exerted herself. Everyone was welcomed into their home at Christmas and nobody left without a present.

Sandra walked upstairs and opened the chest of drawers and took out two presents and gave them to her son.

'Oh mum! You don't have to do this, they don't want a present,' her youngest son Alan said.
'I know that, but at Christmas time, whoever comes into this house leaves with a present. Just humour me will you. It's our tradition.'
'Alright, but you don't have to do this, we're adults now.'
'Just humour me.'
'Alright mum, love you, I'd better go, I think that's them at the door.'

'Are you alright love,' Steve asked as he cuddled his wife.
'Of course, why do you ask that?'
'Do you know how much I love you?'
'I love you too,' she said happily, and she kissed him on the lips, and he closed the bedroom door.

Alan opened the door to his friends and gave them the presents, and the joy he saw on their faces made him smile, then suddenly, he understood why his mother did what she did and decided, that he would carry on with the tradition when he had children.

After all, nobody should ever be left out at Christmas, no matter what people thought about them.

Printed in Great Britain
by Amazon